The Realest Killaz 3

Lock Down Publications and Ca$h

Presents

The Realest Killaz 3

A Novel by *Tranay Adams*

Lock Down Publications

P.O. Box 944
Stockbridge, Ga 30281

First Edition December 2020
Printed in the United States of America

Lock Down Publications
Like our page on Facebook: Lock Down Publications @ www.facebook.com/lockdownpublications.ldp
Cover design and layout by: **Dynasty Cover Me**
Book interior design by: **Shawn Walker**
Edited by: **Nuel Uyi**

Stay Connected with Us!

Text **LOCKDOWN** to 22828 to stay up-to-date with new releases, sneak peaks, contests and more…

Thank you!

Submission Guideline.

Submit the first three chapters of your completed manuscript to ldpsubmissions@gmail.com, subject line: Your book's title. The manuscript must be in a .doc file and sent as an attachment. Document should be in Times New Roman, double spaced and in size 12 font. Also, provide your synopsis and full contact information. If sending multiple submissions, they must each be in a separate email.

Have a story but no way to send it electronically? You can still submit to LDP/Ca$h Presents. Send in the first three chapters, written or typed, of your completed manuscript to:

LDP: Submissions Dept
P.O. Box 944
Stockbridge, Ga 30281

DO NOT send original manuscript. Must be a duplicate.

Provide your synopsis and a cover letter containing your full contact information.

Thanks for considering LDP and Ca$h Presents.

Prologue

Madrid crooned "Ain't That a Kick in The Head?" by Dean Martin while on his knees in his vegetable garden, planting seeds that would eventually produce lettuce. Once he was done, he stuck the trowel he'd used to dig up the dirt into his back pocket, and picked up the watering can. He walked down the rows of carrots, tomatoes, peppers, eggplants, green onions, beans, squash and radishes, showering them.

How lucky can one guy be?
I kissed her and she kissed me
Like the fella once said
Ain't that a kick in the head?

There was something about raising his own vegetable garden that was therapeutic for Madrid. It was his favorite thing to do in his free time. It brought meaning to his life and mellowed him out. At fifty-nine years old, he was a retired hit-man. He made his bones at twelve years old within the Blood Brothers Cartel, taking the soldiers of rival cartels off their feet for his boss. He wound up being the shot-caller's chief enforcer. The soldier his boss called on when he wanted to make sure some knuckleheads got their chance to soar with the angels. Madrid had been putting in work for his organization for forty-four years. When called upon, there wasn't an assignment he didn't complete.

A beautiful, ripe, red tomato caught Madrid's eye. He sat the watering can down and plucked the tomato free, wiping it on the leg of his pants. He took a bite out of it, and its juices squirted inside of his mouth, dripping off his chin. He savored its delicious taste, and munched on a mouthful. Feeling sweat about to drip off his brow, Madrid snatched off his sun hat and whipped out the red bandana from his back pocket. He used the bandana to wipe the perspiration from his forehead, before tucking it back into his back pocket and slapping his sun hat back on his head.

Hearing the telephone ringing, Madrid headed back inside his house, munching on the tomato. Seeing who it was on the caller identification screen, his brows furrowed. He wondered why his former boss, Ignacio, was calling him. Instantly, he figured there was something wrong since they rarely spoke to each other. It wasn't on the account of Ignacio having done something wrong. It was the simple fact that since Madrid had left that lifestyle, he didn't want to be around anyone still in it. The game was addictive, and he didn't want to be sucked back into it. Having devoted a few decades to it, he was lucky to have escaped without a life sentence or death. Something told him that if he ever decided to step back into that world, he wouldn't leave without becoming a victim to those vices. With that thought, he decided not to answer the call, and sat the telephone down. As soon as he did, in two swift motions, he pulled the chrome pistol from his waist line and spun around. Dropping down to one bending knee, he aimed and fired on the two cartel soldiers behind him.

Blocka, blocka, blocka!

The first one hollered aloud, as he fell against the wall and dropped his M-16. Before the third bullet could collide with the first one's body, Madrid was putting three in the second soldier, dropping him as well. Madrid moved in on the soldiers with his pistol, swaying back and forth between them. If they made any sudden moves, then he was going to give them head-shots. Madrid kicked the assault rifles away from the soldier's reach. They lay where they were, wincing with mashed bullets stuck to their bullet-proof vests.

"Who sent chu mothafuckaz, huh? I suggest you speak now before I send you to hell!" Madrid threatened with his face twisted angrily.

Suddenly, there was the sound of clapping coming from the other side of the room. Madrid swung his pistol around in that direction, prepared to open up on anyone there who posed a threat. A moment later, Ignacio rounded the corner inside of the living room, clapping his hands and smiling devilishly. He had been left horribly disfigured from the explosion of the grenade Joaquin had thrown at him and his soldiers years ago. His left eye was milk white, and the left side of his face had been awfully burned. He'd grown out his hair to cover as much of the left side of his face as he could. It was his insecurity. He'd put a bullet into anyone who'd stare at him too long, feeling they were thinking the worse of him.

"The old man has still got it, I see," Ignacio said with regard to Madrid taking out his two soldiers so fast. "That's good. That's very, very good, my friend because I am going to need to render your skills really soon." Ignacio pulled out a cigar and sparked it up. While he was doing this, one of the two soldiers that Madrid had gunned down helped his comrade to his feet; they picked up their M-16s, taking up either side of Ignacio.

Madrid lowered his pistol to his side, and sat on the arm of his couch. He took a deep breath and looked up at Ignacio. "I've been retired for—what? Three years now? Ignacio, I'ma old man now, the murder game is a young man's game. You know that, poppa."

"Indeed." Ignacio blew smoke from out of his mouth. "But youth doesn't compare to experience and skill. Both of which you possess. Besides, I've come here with an incentive that I'm sure will, shall we say, motivate you?" Ignacio looked to his soldiers and said something to them in Spanish. They nodded and disappeared from the living room.

A minute later, they came rolling out wheelbarrows filled with stacks of blue face one hundred dollar bills, which they dumped onto the living room floor. Madrid wasn't sure, but he estimated a total of one million dollars as he looked the cash over. The retired hit-man made a pretty penny under the cartel's reign of terror, but he'd never seen a million dollars all at once. When it came to money, he wouldn't turn down anything but his collar. Besides, only a fool would turn down this kind of loot when someone poured it into his lap.

"What do I have to do for this?" Madrid pointed to the money the soldiers had poured out onto his living room floor.

"I thought you'd never ask." Ignacio smiled harder, knowing Madrid was interested in earning the loot at his feet. "I want chu to track down Joaquin Torres and bring me his fucking head back so I can put it on the wall alongside all of the other cockroaches that wronged me." He scowled and clenched his jaws when he mentioned Joaquin. Inside of his office, back at his villa, he had a collection of severed heads of men that had gotten on his bad side, all of which were dipped in pure gold and kept as memorabilia.

"You still have a hard-on for that pendejo, Ignacio? It's been years now."

"I know that, and no one has managed to find him," Ignacio retorted. "I not only want to avenge my familia, but I want to quiet the noises I've been hearing amongst my men. You see, they still seem to think that I had something to do with my parents' murders since Joaquin is still out there—alive. I figure the only way to quiet them is to bring them the head of the man solely responsible for poppy and mommy's death."

"Wouldn't it be easier to just kill the asshole that's running his mouth?"

"We've done that before with Javier, and that still didn't shut them up."

"Javier?" Madrid frowned up. He couldn't recall who in the hell Javier was. He scratched his temple with the barrel of his pistol, trying to recall the man in question.

Ignacio smiled and shook his head. "Madrid, you've killed so many men that you've forgotten about Javier, haven't you?" Ignacio laughed and looked at his soldiers. They laughed as well. "Allow me to remind you—" he took a pull off the end of his cigar, and blew out a cloud of smoke. He then went on to tell Madrid about the day he murdered Javier for running his big ass mouth.

***

"I'm sorry, jefe, I'm really sorry." Javier trembled as if he was freezing cold. His eyes were pink, and his cheeks were wet from crying. He knew that he was dead-ass wrong for gossiping among the other soldiers. He'd told them that he'd heard that Ignacio was really the one behind the murder of his parents. That he was jealous of the love they shared with Joaquin, and taking Mateo out would leave him to reign supreme over the Blood Brothers Inc. Cartel. Although he was telling the god's honest truth, it didn't matter; that information was something that Ignacio didn't want getting out there. So, Javier opening his loose mouth signed and dated his own Death Certificate. The young soldier knew his time being alive was limited, so he was trying to say whatever he could to prolong the inevitable. "P—please, forgive me. I—I was drunk." He snatched his dingy old Kansas City Chiefs snapback off his head, and held it with both his hands, begging. He wore a faded red T-shirt and a red bandana around his neck, cowboy-style.

Ignacio stood there, staring into the eyes of his pitiful cousin. He couldn't believe that he would betray him as he did. His own flesh and blood had drawn a knife and stabbed him in the back with it. He, Javier and Joaquin had all grown up together, so Javier knew how much he hated Joaquin. The two of them were more like brothers than cousins, so he'd confided in him his deepest, darkest secrets. So for him to get drunk and go blabbing off what he'd entrusted him with was blasphemy, and there wasn't any chance of him getting his forgiveness.

"You broke my heart, Javier," Ignacio told him, teary eyed.

"Ignacio, I know," Javier began. "I fucked up, bro. I really fucked up, and I'm sorry." He cried and sniffled, wiping his dripping eyes with his curled finger.

Feeling like his pleading was getting through to his cousin, Javier took a step closer to him to plead his case some more, but Ignacio held up his hand. Javier stopped cold in his tracks, and lowered his head pitifully. Big teardrops fell from his eyes, and splashed on the floor.

"No. You've said some evil, hurtful things about me—Now, I've gotta turn my back on you," Ignacio stated firmly, and then he turned his back to Javier. When Javier approached him again, Madrid came up from behind him and tapped him on his shoulder with his gold, skeletal claw-like hand, which had razor sharp talons on its finger tips. Startled, Javier turned around to him. Growling, Madrid attacked him savagely with his gold talons, swiping across Javier's abdomen twice and spilling his insides onto the floor. Wide eyed, mouth hanging open, Javier looked up at Madrid. Swiftly, Madrid slashed him across the face twice, and then across the jugular.

"Aaaaaaah—gaggggg—gaaaagg—" Javier hollered

aloud in agony as the final slash across his neck spun him around. His face had deep blood gashes in it. His left eyeball was missing, blood and other colorful gunk oozing out of its socket. The slash across his jugular spilled buckets of blood down his shirt. With his good eye, he looked at Ignacio's back accusingly. As he reached out for him, his eye rolled to its white, and he suddenly dropped dead. Madrid stood over him, watching as the blood poured out of his wounds and onto the floor. Madrid held his talons out beside him, as they dripped blood. One of the talons had half of Javier's left eyeball stuck to the tip of it. Using his teeth, Madrid grabbed the half of an eyeball off his talon and spat it on the floor, beside Javier's corpse.

"Excellent work, Madrid," Ignacio told his chief enforcer, as he walked over to his desk and picked up a bottle of D'usse. He pulled open his desk drawer and sat a glass down on top of it. "Now, would you be so kind as to send a couple of fellows in to dispose of Javier's body and clean up this mess?" He poured his glass halfway full, picked it up, and sat down in his executive office chair. As he took a sip from his glass, Madrid nodded and headed for the door to carry out his command.

***

"Now, I remember," Madrid told him and rose from the arm of the couch, tucking his pistol into the front of his pants. "So, how much is my take once I bring your brother's head to you?"

"Please, don't insult me." Ignacio's face twisted hatefully. "That monkey is no brother of mine. We don't have any blood ties. And as far as your take—this one million dollars lying on the floor of your living room is yours, just for entertaining this conversation. You'll receive another one million dollars one I have that mayate's head sitting on my trophy self."

Madrid nodded understandingly and said, "Okay, when do I leave for—Wait a minute, where the hell am I going? You failed to mention it."

"Los Angeles," Ignacio said. "The tunnel inside of my parents' house leads straight to the City of Angels. It will take you there. It's up to you to decide if you'll be taking some of my men along, or if you'll be flying solo on this mission. As for when you'll leave, the sooner the better."

"Right. Well, gemme a couple of days to get things situated and to get someone to tend to my garden while I'm gone."

"Very well, Madrid—Just call me when you're ready," Ignacio told him, making his hand into the shape of a telephone, and holding it to his ear.

"Sure thing."

"How about a hug, old man? It's been a while since I've seen you," Ignacio said with a smile, and opened his arms to receive Madrid. Madrid hugged him and patted him on his back. "You get that mothafucka for me, Madrid. You get that pinche negrito's head and bring it back to me for mi familia. You hear me?" Teary eyed, he held Madrid at arm's length when he posed the question. Suddenly, tears slid down his cheeks unevenly. Madrid nodded. Ignacio wiped his eyes and flashed him a smile, patting him on the shoulder. He then kissed him on the cheek and headed for the door, signaling for his soldiers to follow him.

***

Madrid opted to take a first-class flight rather than use

Ignacio's underground tunnel. When his plane landed, he caught an Uber to his daughter Elizabeth's house. He told her, days prior, he was coming to town to visit her and the kids since he hadn't seen them since Eric's funeral. Detective Eric Salazar was Elizabeth's husband and the father of her five children. He'd unfortunately been killed when he'd tracked down a suspect in several rapes and murders of prostitutes. A shoot-out ensued between the serial killa, Eric and his partner—Detective Paul Barrett. When the smoke cleared, Detective Barrett was the last man standing, while Eric and the notorious Figueroa Street Body Snatcher were dead.

Since then, Madrid's only contact with his family had been through *Zoom*. He missed his family awfully, and figured he'd catch up with them while he was in town. Getting reacquainted with his loved ones would also give him time to make a few phone calls so he could find out where Joaquin was holed up. The sooner he put him out of his misery, the sooner he could head back home to collect the other half of his money.

It was five o'clock in the evening when Madrid found himself seated at the dinner table with his daughter and grandchildren. He was enjoying his time with his family so much he wished he'd decided to come see them sooner. He was creating memories with them that he hoped they would cherish their time together as much as he would.

"I'd like to propose a toast to my oldest grandson, Junior," Madrid raised his glass of wine. He was sitting at the head of the dinner table, while Elizabeth was sitting at the other end. The rest of the table was surrounded by her five children. They had two boys and three girls. "For bringing a championship to his high school basketball team, here's to this championship and many more to come.

Hopefully the rest will be won on the floors of the NBA—to Junior."

"To Junior!" everyone else said in unison, touching their glasses and cups together before taking a drink.

"You don't have to gloat, Stilts—You can take your trophy off the table now," Dee Dee said to her brother, annoyingly. At fourteen, she was the oldest out of the three girls, and looked the most like their mother out of all of the children.

Junior took his trophy off the table top, kissed it, smiled, and sat it on the floor beside his leg. He was sixteen years old and stood a dominating six-foot-six. He wore his hair in a tapered fade with a part cut in the side of it. Oddly enough, he was the spitting image of his grandfather, Madrid, except he had golden-brown skin. Due to the young man's height, he was affectionately called Stilts—on and off the basketball court.

"Happy now?" Junior taunted and slapped hands with his younger brother, Stink, who was laughing his ass off.

"What are you laughing at, with your water-head?" Dee Dee cut her eyes at Stink.

"Your momma has a water-head," Stink shot back. He was fifteen and three inches shorter than Junior. He wore his hair in a Mohawk, and looked a lot like Madrid. He'd gotten his nickname from his father due to him consistently having a smelly, shitty pamper. Later, the family found out that it was on the account of him being lactose-intolerant—which gave him diarrhea.

Dee Dee angrily shot to her feet with her fists balled at her sides. "Say something else about my momma again, I dare you!" she said threateningly to Stink.

"I dare you too," Inez chimed in with a mouthful, grinning.

"I second that." Laura added her two cents.

"That's enough. You two shut it and zip it up." Elizabeth chastised her two youngest daughters while wagging her finger at them.

"Dee Dee, sit cho lil' self down, we all got the same momma," Stilts said after taking a drink of his cup of fruit punch. "You hopping up out cho seat like he's some fool offa the street, relax."

Frowning, Elizabeth told Dee Dee: "D'Autra, you're entire too bello to be acting the way you are right now. Take a seat."

Madrid looked around at his family, smiling. Elizabeth's forehead wrinkled, as she wondered what was up with him.

"What are you smiling about, papi?" Elizabeth asked curiously, and took a bite of her food.

"Aw, nothing really, it just nice to be around family again, is all," Madrid replied, smiling harder. "I really missed you guys."

"Awww, papi." Elizabeth smiled, as her eyes watered emotionally. For the first time in her life, she'd seen her father become teary eyed. Elizabeth loved her old man to death. Mexico had become deadly as fuck, so he'd given her mother a big bag and gathered all of the necessary paperwork for them to move to America. Although her mother and he weren't together any more, that didn't stop him from playing the role of protector and provider. They had a highly skilled bodyguard with them twenty-four-seven, day in, day out, and more than enough money was sent to them every month. Madrid made sure his daughter and her mother had a roof over their heads, food in the fridge, a nice car to drive, and anything else they needed.

"Family hug!" Elizabeth called out with her hands in the air. She bounced to her feet and darted over to Madrid. She hugged him, and kissed him on his cheek. The younger girls crawled into his lap, kissing and hugging him. Dee kissed him on the cheek, and hugged him as well. Right after, Stilts and Stink dropped their forks onto their plates, and made their way over to their grandfather. They hugged and kissed him as well.

Although Madrid had been conditioned to not show any love or remorse, over the years he'd found himself vulnerable when things concerned his family. They were truly his weakness. In fact, at that moment, a single tear drop emerged and slid down his cheek. Elizabeth wiped her father's lone tear away and kissed him again, hugging him tightly. Elizabeth grabbed her selfie-stick, and they took several pictures of her family together. She also took several more of herself and her father, then her children and her father.

After taking the pictures, the family went on to finish their meals. Afterwards, Elizabeth and the girls tended to the kitchen table, and washed the dishes. Stink took out the trash, and shot around with the basketball in the backyard. Madrid sipped a Corona while Stilts showed him different portraits on the shelves and on the wall, telling him stories behind it.

"Who are the white kid and the white dude with you, your brother and father here?" Madrid asked Stilts about the portrait on the mantle. The picture had all of them wearing hats and fishing gear. They were smiling while holding up their fishing poles and the fish they'd caught.

"That's my best friend Aaron and his father. His father was a detective, too. They worked together as partners. They were best friends too." Junior smiled as he gave his grandfather this information.

Detective, huh? I can probably use this guy to get some

information on Joaquin for me. He could definitely gemme his past and present addresses. At the very least, I could getta line onna fiancée, girlfriend or someone he's affiliated with that could tell me where he is, Madrid thought, as he took a drink from his Corona and swallowed it down.

"Are you and Aaron still friends?" Madrid asked Junior.

"We aren't as close as we once were," Junior admitted. "We kinda grew apart. He started leaning more toward the streets while I chose the path that my talent is leading me down. The streets and the road I'm traveling down do not mix, and I'm sure as hell notta 'bouta allow anyone to mess up my chances of going where I wanna go in life."

Madrid nodded understandingly. He was glad to hear that his grandson was focused and determined to make his dream a reality. "What is your best bud up to these days?" he asked him innocently. He was just trying to find out where he could possibly locate him so he could use him as a bargaining chip.

"If I hadda guess, I'd say *being a juvenile delinquent*. I hardly ever see 'em at school anymore. He and new crowda buddies spend a lotta time at that park you used to take me and Stink up to when you'd come visit. I'd see him and his lil' clique up there a lotta times, smoking, drinking and doing tricks on their skateboards when I'd drive past there. I hate to admit it but my boy has turned out to be sucha fucking loser. Excuse my French, grandpa. I don't mean any disrespect."

Madrid smiled and gripped Junior's shoulder. "It's okay, son, don't worry about it." He told patted him on his back.

Junior's cellular suddenly rang, and he looked at it. A smile stretched across his face. "Grandpa, I've gotta take this."

"Girlfriend, huh?" Madrid grinned and took a sip of his Corona. Junior smiled and nodded before going into his bedroom, slamming the door shut behind him.

Madrid looked over his shoulder and saw that Elizabeth and the girls were still busy with the dishes. He picked up the portrait, and carried it inside the guest room he was going to be staying in while in Los Angeles. After locking the door, he plopped down on the bed and put on his blue-tooth. He hit up an arms dealer of his that didn't live too far from his daughter's crib. He listened to the phone ringing, as he opened up the portrait and removed the picture inside of it. Holding the picture before his eyes, he looked it over and he began talking to his dealer.

"What's up? I'm in town. I was hoping to come by and see you. Is the store still open? Good." Madrid said to his dealer, still staring at Aaron in the picture.

Chapter 1

Murtaugh was sitting outside of God's crib, listening to Cypress Hill's "How I Could Just Kill a Man", while smoking a joint. His eyelids were shut, and he was nodding , zoning out. You know, getting into the mind frame of a cold-blooded killa. Murtaugh had his hands in many deaths, being a crooked ass corrections officer, but it was rare for him to get his hands dirty. He'd gotten busy at Tomas's mansion with his goons, and here he was again— about to murder an entire family. He'd convinced himself that what he was doing was a necessary evil. Once they'd gotten rid of God, Billie and Charity, Joaquin would get sole custody of Annabelle. Then they'd have full reign over the city, and they could move their product without interference from other drug crews. Joaquin was already in the midst of making a deal with the police to look the other way while they did their thing, so in a minute they wouldn't have them to knock their hustle.

Still nodding to the music, Murtaugh mashed out what was left of his joint and slipped his hands inside a pair of black leather gloves. He took a Steyr AUG assault rifle from underneath the driver's seat, and chambered a live round into it. After sticking two fully loaded magazines for the automatic weapon in the pocket of his jacket, Murtaugh pulled a black ski-mask down over his face, and hopped out of the car. Shutting the door as quietly as he could behind him, he looked up and down the street for any oncoming cars. When he didn't see anyone coming, he jogged across the street—ready to leave a murder scene that would surely make every news channel in the country.

***

Billie was engrossed in the *Blood & Water* episode she was watching on television when the doorbell rang. Her forehead crinkled as she wondered who it might be. She knew it wasn't God because he would have just used his key to get in. With that in mind, Billie walked toward the front door, scratching under her arm.

"Who is it?" Billie called out to whoever was at the door.

Buratatatatatatatatatat!

Bullets chewed up the front door and sent splinters flying. Billie dropped to the floor and looked to the hallway, seeing Charity and Annabelle there looking concerned.

"Y'all go to y'all room and lock the door! Go now, now!" Billie called out to them in a panic. As soon as the girls darted back to their bedroom, the front door rattled from a tyrannical force that was trying to get inside. Billie scrambled to her feet and took off toward the hallway. *Boom!* The front door swung inward, and Murtaugh rushed in, lifting and pointing his German assault rifle. He pulled the trigger and the gun vibrated, spitting fire. The bullets missed Billie by an inch, as she hung a left inside of the hallway. She placed her back against the hallway. Breathing huskily, she wiped her sweaty forehead with the back of her hand. She looked to the hallway closet, and then to the bathroom. She patted her pocket, and felt something small and shaped like a rectangle. She pulled it out of her pocket in a hurry, and held it up before her eyes. It was a yellow Bic lighter.

Billie looked to the entrance of the hallway, and heard Murtaugh slowly approaching. She knew she had to make her move fast before it was too late. Murtaugh placed his back against the wall right before you entered the hallway.

He crept his way toward the entrance of the corridor, and then spun into it, sub-machine gun up and ready to fire. His brows furrowed in confusion behind his ski-mask when he didn't see Billie anywhere in sight. Spotting the closet door cracked open, a smile spread across his lips, and he advanced in the direction of the closet. As soon as he'd gotten close enough, he kicked the closet's door closed and sprayed it full of holes.

"Got cha, bitch!" Murtaugh said happily, as he ejected the magazine from his Steyr AUG assault rifle and reloaded it, cocking a live round in its head. He snatched the door open, expecting Billie to fall flat out into the hallway dead, but she hadn't. His eyelids narrowed into slits, and he wondered where she was. He felt around inside of the closet for the drawstring for the light bulb. Grasping it, he yanked it, and the light popped on. There wasn't anything stored inside besides a stack of cardboard boxes which were labeled with a black Sharpie marker. Suddenly, his eyes bulged when he'd heard the bathroom door creak as it was opened from behind him. He spun around, ready to cut Billie down, but he was in for a surprise of a lifetime when he saw her standing there. She held up the blue flame of her lighter and a can of air freshener behind it. She scowled and clenched her jaws as she sprayed the freshener. The flammable substance mingled with the flame and acted as a blow torch. A fireball erupted forward and set Murtaugh ablaze.

"Aaaaaaaaaaah!" Murtaugh screamed in unbearable pain, as the fire spread from the top of his head to the beginning of his belt. He spun around in circles, bumping into the hallway walls, firing his German machine gun, sporadically.

Shit, I hope the girls are okay, Billie thought, as Murtaugh fired his weapon. She watched as he eventually dropped it and fell to the carpeted floor. He rolled around on the floor until he'd put out the fire, and laid still on his back, billowing with smoke. The only thing left ablaze was his left arm.

***

God dropped off the work to all the cooks on his payroll except Ms. Jones. He had expected to be in and out of her crib so he could head back to his own to get some sleep, but she wasn't answering her front door. Repeatedly, he hit up the cell phone he'd given her, and was sent straight to voicemail. He tried to leave her a message, but her mail box was full. God decided to try her front door again. Once again, he didn't get an answer; so he traveled to the side of the house, and tried to peek inside through the window. He could see the light inside of the kitchen was still on, but he couldn't see anyone moving around.

He decided to try his luck with the back door. He tossed his duffle bag over and climbed the gate, jumping down into the back yard. Snatching up his duffle bag, he made his way upon the back porch and tried the doorknob. His forehead creased, seeing that the door was already open.

Something is up! Momma Jones never leaves her shit unlocked!

God slipped the strap of the duffle bag over his neck, and pulled his gun from his waistline. He cocked it, and slipped inside the back door, moving through the kitchen with the skill of a police officer. The kitchen looked normal, but he could see from where he was standing that the living room looked like a cyclone had been through it. God could tell a struggle had taken place—from the flipped over sofa, the toppled lamp, the broken vase, the knocked over coffee table, the portrait hanging crooked on the wall, and the cobweb in the flat-screen television set.

What a tough old bird! From the look of things she put up one hell of a fight, God thought, as he looked over the messy living room. *Lemme check out the rest of this house before I get outta here.*

God took a step forward and felt something crack underneath his sneaker. His forehead crinkled as he wondered what he'd stepped on. He removed his sneaker from what he'd stepped on, to uncover Ms. Jones' scorched and scarred crack pipe. He picked it up, and his eyelids narrowed into slits, examining it closely. It still had crack rocks in it that appeared to be melted. That meant Ms. Jones was in the middle of getting high when *whoever* ran up in her crib and kidnapped her.

Yeah, somebody definitely snatched up my OG, that's for damn sure.

God's eyebrows slanted, his nose wrinkled, and he clenched his jaws. He was so angry he squeezed the crack pipe in his fist until it snapped, crackled and popped. He threw its remains aside, brushed his hand off on the leg of his jeans, and made his way out of the house, determined to find out what happened to Ms. Jones.

I know who has her—that bitch-ass nigga Joaquin. I love Momma Jones. Since I've been running these streets she's always been like a mother to me. I swear on everything I love—if homeboy has harmed so much as a hair on her head, I'ma kill his vindictive ass.

God made his way out of the back door of Ms. Jones' crib, tossed his duffle bag over the gate, and then scaled it. He jumped down to the driveway, snatched his duffle bag back up, and made his way across the street to his car. After depositing his bag of work inside of the spare tire compartment in the trunk, he hopped into his whip, and drove off. Hanging a few corners and driving up a residential block, he found himself at a red stoplight. He took the time to fish what was left of his blunt out of the ashtray, and stuck it between his full lips. Leaning back in the driver seat, he pulled out a lighter from his pocket, and ignited a blue flame with it. He was bringing the flame of his lighter to the tip of his bleezy when he caught a glimpse of Asad in the backseat.

"What the fuck?" God blurted in shock, as his eyes bulged and his mouth flung open. His brows crinkled, and his head snapped around to the back seat. He didn't see anyone sitting there, so he looked to both sides of the floor. Nothing, or no one, was there. He took a deep breath.

Man, a nigga tripping hard as a mothafucka, God thought, as he dropped his head and massaged the bridge of his nose. The honking of a car horn startled him, and he looked out of the back window, seeing the latest Chrysler 300. It was maroon, and sitting on stock rims, with tinted windows.

"Alright, alright, al-fucking-right," God said to the driver of the vehicle, as if he or she could hear him. He turned around to a green traffic light and drove through it, lighting up his blunt. Once its cherry was glowing, he tossed the lighter aside on the front passenger seat, and took a couple of drags from his bleezy. He blew out a cloud of smoke, and scratched his temple with his thumb, crossing the intersection. His mind drifted to a couple of years ago when he'd met Asad. It tripped him out because he'd almost popped the young nigga, but he was glad that he hadn't.

***

"What's the science on this nigga? Who he rolling

with?" God asked from the back seat. He was peering from between the front seats and through the windshield at who he didn't know was Asad, who was hustling on the corner.

"Mannnn, as far as I can see, homie out here on some solo shit," Buck Wild said from behind the wheel of the bullet-proof Suburban.

"You sho, big dog?" God looked at him.

"Yeah, we sho, shawty, we did a lil' intell'—He's the only lil' jit out here from six in the a.m. 'til six at night," Country interjected from the front passenger seat.

"Unh huh, the mothafucka getting it, too, clocking hella dollars. At least from what I can see."

"It's okay, 'cause I'ma 'bouta get his ass the fuck up outta here," Buck Wild said, pulling black leather gloves over his hands, and flexed his fingers inside of them. He then pulled his Desert Eagle from underneath the front passenger seat, and chambered a dead round inside of its head. "Alright, God, you can hop in the other truck and pull off. Me and Country got it from here—" Buck Wild looked over his shoulder into the back seat at God, who looked like he was thinking something over as he stared out of the backseat window, massaging his chin.

It's beena long while since a nigga put in some work. I know as a boss I'm 'pose to let my goons handle the grunt work, but every now and again you gotta remind yo' niggaz that you started where they were and climbed yo' way to the top. Yo' spot wasn't just given to you. Besides, it's time I remind these niggaz that I ain't never too big to lay my gangsta down!

After making up his mind about how he was going to handle things, God looked to Buck Wild and said, "Nah, I got this one faded, Buck."

"Huh?" Buck Wild's eyebrows rose with surprise. He

couldn't remember the last time he saw God splash a nigga.

"I said, 'I got it, my nigga'. Lemme get that piece." God slipped his hands inside a pair of black leather gloves and flexed his fingers inside of them, just like Buck Wild had done. He then slipped a pair of black sunglasses onto his face and threw his hood over his head. Next, he outstretched his hand for Buck Wild to give him his Desert Eagle.

"You can't be serious, dog; fuck is the use of God having angels if he is not gonna use them to spread his gospel?" Country said, as he held up two pistols. One was a chrome .44 magnum revolver while the other was a black .45 automatic.

Ignoring Country, God took the Desert Eagle from Buck Wild. He checked the magazine of the chrome blower, and made sure it was fully loaded. He then slid over to the back door behind Buck Wild's seat. While he was doing this, Country was hitting up the driver of the other truck to let him know that there had been a change of plans, and that he could roll out now.

God popped open the back door and jumped out, shutting the door quietly behind him. He hunched over and held his blower low at his side, moving in on the opposition fast and sneakily. The entire time, Asad had his back to him serving crackheads that didn't seem to notice him, thanks to the cloak of darkness. Asad had just served his last crackhead and stuffed the wrinkled bills inside his pocket. When he turned around, God whacked him across the head with the handle of his Desert Eagle, dropping him to his hands and knees. While he was in this position, God kicked and stomped the shit out of him, reminding him whose block he was hustling on.

"Ol' busta-ass mothafucka!" God kicked him hard as shit in his stomach, dropping him on his torso. He then

pushed him over onto his back and found him not only wincing, but bleeding at the corner of his mouth. When Asad moved to draw his blower from his waistline, God pressed his sneaker against his hand, pinning his gun to his waist. "Proverbs 6:12-18. A troublemaker and a villain, who goes about with a corrupt mouth, who winks maliciously with his eye, signals with his feet and motions with his fingers, who plots evil with deceit in his heart—he always stirs up conflict. Therefore, disaster will overtake him in an instant; he will suddenly be destroyed—without remedy!" God's eyebrows sloped, and he clenched his jaws, leveling his Desert Eagle at Asad's forehead. He was about to pull the trigger, until he noticed the gold dog-tags hanging around his neck. One was of a beautiful little girl, and the other was of an attractive young lady. God wasn't sure, but something told him that this was his girlfriend and daughter. Asad's forehead wrinkled, and he wondered why God hadn't given his black ass a halo yet.

"Is that your family hanging around your neck?" God asked him.

"Look, nigga, if you gon' kill me then kill me, but I'm not telling you where my people lay their heads, alright?" Asad said as he mad-dogged him. He was ready to face the consequences of his actions. He knew he shouldn't have been hustling on that corner, but he had a family to take care of. He had to do what he had to do to take care of them.

"Either you tell me whether that's your family or not. Or, I'ma leave you as a stain on this sidewalk. You've got 'til the count of three: One—two—"

"Okay, okay," Asad told him in a panic. "Yeah, that's my fam, my fiancée and my daughter."

"How old is lil' mama?"

"She just turned two."

God nodded understandingly and said, "That's why you're out here hustling, huh?"

Asad was silent for a minute before answering. "Yeah. They're the reason why I'm out here taking penitentiary chances. I gotta do what I gotta do to take care of 'em."

God took a deep breath and lowered his blower. He then picked up Asad's gun and tucked them both at the small of his back. He extended his hand toward him, and Asad looked at it and then up into his eyes. He pondered on whether he should take his hand or not. This could have been a trap, but something told him that homie was sincere. Asad grasped God's hand, and God pulled him up to his feet. Asad dusted himself off and stood upright. He didn't know what to expect, especially seeing the two dark figures—Buck Wild and Country—approaching him.

"What's up, man?" Asad looked from the approaching figures then back to God. He was trying to see what he had in mind to do to him. His first mind had told him to bust him in his mouth and take off running. He shook that idea from his head, when he realized God would probably gun him down before he made it halfway up the block. Still, he had to do something. He wasn't about to just let these niggaz do whatever they wanted to him. With the thought of death being in his near future, Asad slowly slipped his hand into his back pocket, where he kept his switchblade.

"Lil' bruh," God called after Asad, which startled him. He'd already seen his movements, and knew he planned on making a move. "Don't try it, fam, my goons walking up right now and will chop you down. I don't wanna see that happen to you, lil' bruh." Asad nodded understandingly. "Go ahead and hand me however many rocks you got left." He extended his glove hand, showing Asad his palm. Asad pulled out five off-white crack rocks and handed them to him.

God dropped those shit at his feet, stomping and mashing them out under his sneaker. Asad looked at him like he was fucking crazy.

"My nigga, those are twenty dollar rocks you just mashed into the ground," Asad said, looking down at the ruined crack rocks mashed against the pavement. "That's a hunnit dollars down the fucking drain."

"Come on, you're gonna take a lil' ride with me," God told Asad.

"You good, God?" Country asked him. Buck Wild was standing beside him. They both were wearing menacing expressions across their faces and eyeballing Asad like they wanted to cause harm to him.

"Yeah, everything is everything. Homeboy here is just gonna—" God frowned up, as he recalled he'd never gotten Asad's name. So, he turned to him. "What's yo' name, young nigga?"

"Asad."

God introduced himself, and then he introduced Buck Wild and Country. "Asad is gonna roll with us to get something to eat while we discuss this business proposition with 'em," God told his angels. "How'd you like Roscoe's Chicken & Waffles?"

"Shit, I love Roscoe's," Asad admitted.

"Good. That's where we're headed then. Let's roll." God motioned for everyone to follow him as he headed back toward the Suburban. Country and Buck Wild fell in line behind him while Asad was hesitant to come along. Seeing this, God looked over his shoulder and said, "Come on, nigga, I thought chu said you were hungry."

"I am," Asad replied. "Wait up." He jogged after the trio to catch up.

That night, they pigged out at Roscoe's, and God offered

Asad a job within his organization. Asad accepted the offer. God paid for the check. He then dropped Asad the blue face Benji for the crack he destroyed, and laid two racks on him for free. From that day forth, God and Asad rolled together tough. They looked at each other as brothers while Buck Wild and Country looked at him like a nephew. Everyone had become tightly knit, and you'd hardly see any of them without the other.

***

P-Diddy's "I'll Be Missing You" was playing on the radio as God drove alone. Listening to the music seemed to put him in a grieving mood, and left him in an emotionally vulnerable state.

Life ain't always what it seem to be (uh-uh)
Words can't express what you mean to me
Even though you're gone, we still a team
Through your family, I'll fulfill your dream (that's right)

God's eyes pooled with water, while thinking about Asad, and big teardrops fell from them. Sniffling, he took the smoldering blunt from between his lips and blew out a cloud of smoke. Wiping his dripping eyes with the same hand he held his blunt in, the song brought more tears to his eyes, and he started spitting the lyrics along with Sean Combs.

"In the future, can't wait to see/ If you open up the gates for me—" God said, reciting the bars. He knew the lyrics to the song by heart. And the more of them he spat, the more he cried. He turned the volume of the song up, and the bass rattled his speakers. He shut his eyelids, bobbed his head to the beat, and drummed his hand on the steering wheel, becoming lost in the music. He was feeling it. All of the ups and downs he and Asad shared played inside the theater of his mind, like he was seated center row at a matinee. This very moment he was experiencing was so vivid it was almost like he was there with his little brother again. It was crazy because although it was beautiful, it was also ugly at the same time.

God started drumming the steering wheel harder and spat the words louder. The hook of the song was coming up—which was his favorite part. He couldn't sing for shit, but that wasn't going to stop him from giving it his all. Still crying, he threw his head back and sang with all of his heart and soul.

"Every step I take, every move I make/ Every single day, every time I pray/ I'll be missing you/ Thinkin' of the day, when you went away—" God rested his forehead against his fists, which were wrapped around the steering wheel. His shoulders shuddered, his head bobbed as he cried long and hard, as the song continued to play. He was in the intersection and holding up traffic. Losing Asad had really fucked him up. Now there he was, risking a lifetime behind bars with a gun on him and bricks of dope in the trunk of his car. Angry drivers honked their horns madly for him to move, but he wasn't budging. Some of the drivers drove around him and went on their way, but others couldn't move without him getting out of their way. The driver of a yellow Ford F-Series with red racing stripes hopped out of his whip, slamming its door shut. He was a buff-ass light-skinned brother with a bald head and a long beard. He was wearing a sweat-stained tank top and basketball shorts. It was obvious he'd just left the gym. He cracked his knuckles as he approached the driver's side window of God's whip, looking like he was about to whip some ass. Especially with that scowl plastering his face.

Knock, knock, knock, knock!

"Say, bruh, I don't know what the fuck your problem is but chu needa move your fuckin'—" The rest of the words died in the buff nigga's throat. His eyes widened, and he threw his massive hands in the air, surrendering.

"Back up, back the fuck up! Or, I swear on everything I love I'll blow yo' fucking head off!" God roared so loud and hard that his spit spotted the inside of the driver's window. His eyes were pink, his face was wet, and green snot was threatening to slide over his top lip. He was pointing his blower, which had a silencer on its tip, at the buff mothafucka at his window. He was an emotional wreck, and on the edge. The way he was feeling, he would have definitely blown homeboy's brains out in front of countless witnesses.

"Alright, bro, relax, relax!" the bald-headed dude said, as he slowly stepped back from God's car. Suddenly, he whipped around and ran back to his truck, jumping back inside. Hurriedly, he threw it in reverse and mashed the gas pedal, as he looked over his shoulder. The pick-up sped backwards, and he whipped it around, burning rubber in the opposite direction. On the door of the flatbed in fancy bold letters was *The Pussy Magnet.*

Once the buff-ass dude had gone, God sat his gun aside on the front passenger seat, and placed his forehead back on top of his fists. He cried and cried until the song had gone off, then a commercial played, and he didn't have another tear left in him. Afterwards, he lifted his head up, wiped his wet face and sniffled. Pulling Asad's gold lion head medallion from out of his shirt, he kissed it and looked up to the ceiling of his ride.

"I love you, lil' bro, man, I'll never forget you and I'll keep yo' memory alive," God swore to his deceased comrade. "I got cho shorty, too, dog. On the lives of me and my family, yo' lil' mama ain't gon' ever have to want for nothing." He kissed the lion's head again and tucked it back inside of his shirt. He then put his car in drive and mashed the gas pedal, pulling off. As soon as he was gone, the flow of traffic picked back up, and everything went right back to normal.

Chapter 2

Billie got upon her feet and cautiously approached Murtaugh. Once she'd gotten upon him, she kicked his boot twice, but he didn't move. She assumed he was dead. Relief swept over her entire body. She took a breath and ran her hand down her face.

"Girls, are you okay?" Billie called out to Charity and Annabelle.

"Yes, we're fine," Charity answered.

"Good. Come—" Billie was cut short when Murtaugh kicked her in the stomach, doubling her over. Coming upon his knees, he gave her a backhand punch that sent her flying backward. She crashed to the floor on her back first, and her legs came down after.

Murtaugh's ski-mask was embedded into his burnt face, and his jacket was pressing into his hideously burned body. He was in excruciating pain, but he'd tend to his wounds once he'd completed his mission—assassinating Billie. Murtaugh smacked the burning flames from his left sleeve until he'd extinguished it. When he looked to Billie, she was on her hands and knees, spitting blood on the carpeted floor. Seeing that she was at his mercy, he figured now was as good a time as any to finish her off. He turned around in circles, looking for his German sub-machine gun. His eyes lit up, and a sinister smile spread across his face, seeing the gun at the entrance of the hallway. He picked it up and made sure it was loaded. Turning around to spray Billie, his face balled up in confusion, seeing she'd vanished from where she was.

Hearing hurried footsteps at his left, Murtaugh turned around to Billie charging at him. He went to unload on her, but she kicked the sub-machine gun from out of her path, and the assault rifle went off. She laid hard into him, unleashing a flurry of punches on his torso, landing a crushing overhand right, a left, and jumping up to deliver a spinning kick against his head. Murtaugh dropped his sub-machine gun and swung two haymakers at Billie's head. Billie dodged with ease. She punched either side of his ribcage, and slammed her fist into his gut, causing him to double over. Next, she grasped his shoulders and forced his face downward while driving her knee upward. The blow bloodied his nose and knocked out three of his teeth, leaving his mouth heavily bleeding.

Murtaugh dropped to his hands and knees, bleeding profusely from his wounds. Exhausted, his chest heaved up and down. When he saw Billie going for his sub-machine gun, he had to act fast. Grunting, he launched himself from off the floor, tackled Billie and lifted her up. He carried her inside of the living room, and slammed her down to the floor. She grimaced, and her eyes rolled to their whites.

"I'll give it to you, sweetheart, you're a bad ass assassin just like Joaquin said you were," Murtaugh said, as he straddled her and reached behind his back. "But a bitch is a bitch. I don't care how skilled she is, she's still no match for a man." He drew the hunting knife sheathed at his back and brought it before her eyes. As her vision came into focus from her dizzy spell, she could see her reflection in the shiny blade. She wanted to fight him off, but his attack had knocked the wind out of her and left her weakened. "I'm gonna cut your fucking titties off, then I'm gonna slice ya throat from ear to—" Murtaugh was in the middle of showing Billie how he was going to slice her throat from ear to ear when he was cut down by rapid gunfire. Murtaugh's shoulders danced, as he was struck in either side of his body. He dropped his hunting knife, and looked up at God who was standing in the doorway. He was clutching his .45 with both hands, his head was tilted to the side and his left eye was shut. He lined up the sighting of his blower with Murtaugh's forehead and recited a prayer.

"Grant eternal rest unto him, oh, Lord. And let perpetual light shine upon him. May his soul and the souls of all the departed, through the mercy of God, rest in peace. Amen." God pulled the trigger of his gun; an empty shell casing disengaged, and a hollow-tip bullet rocketed out of its barrel. Sparks flew out behind the bullet, as it ripped through the air like a heat-seeking missile. Before Murtaugh knew it, his head was erupting like a white head zit. Blood and brain fragments flew out the back of his skull, and he leaned all the way back, hands lying on either side of him. He was definitely dead!

Billie kicked him off her and scrambled to her feet, holding her aching back. Wincing, she turned around to Murtaugh, spitting on him and kicking him in his head. She ran over to God and fell into his arms. He held her tightly and rubbed her back, kissing her on top of her head. As badly as she wanted to cry, she fought back her tears. Kershawn had trained her to be cold, calculating and without feeling, when they went up in those mountains. Though that went against her nature, her conditioning helped her combat her emotions. Looking over Billie's shoulder at Murtaugh, God's forehead deepened with lines. He wasn't sure, but he believed he knew who he was. With that in mind, he broke his embrace from Billie and approached him. Kneeling down to him, he started picking off the fabric of the ski-mask that had been embedded into Murtaugh's face. After picking the burnt fabric from off the dead man's charred, face he threw it aside. The more he picked, the more Murtaugh's facial features became visible. After a while, God stopped picking away at the fabric. A shocked expression came across his face, as he realized he knew the man that invaded his home.

"What's the matter, baby?" Billie asked, as she looked from Murtaugh to her husband, with her hands on her hips.

"I—I know this nigga," God told her with his eyes still on Murtaugh, scratching his temple with his gun. He couldn't believe he'd broken inside of his crib and tried to murder Billie. He figured he would have bodied his ass too if he'd been present. Thankfully, he hadn't though.

"How?"

"I hired 'em to knock off someone behind the wall—he's a corrections officer." God stood upright, still looking down at Murtaugh. "Yo' baby daddy just got outta jail not too long ago. I bet my left nut the two of them are connected, and they got acquainted while he was on the inside."

"It's truly a small world."

"Sho' in the fuck is—Listen, take my piece and hide it somewhere inside of our bedroom," God told her, as he passed her his gun. "We've gotta see about getting rid of this fool's body. I know he hadda have driven here, so it's best we get his whip towed so no one will ever know that he's been here."

"Okay." Billie disappeared inside of the hallway to stash the gun inside their bedroom.

"Billie, what's going on? Who were you fighting?" God overheard Charity talking to Billie. The sound of her voice startled him. He didn't want her or Annabelle to see Murtaugh's dead body. His head was on a swivel, as he scanned the living room, looking for something to cover his body with. Spotting a trench coat hanging up on the coat-stand, he snatched it free and draped it over Murtaugh's corpse like a sheet.

"Yes, baby, someone had broken in but I fought 'em off and he ran away," Billie lied smoothly.

"Are you, okay?" Annabelle asked innocently.

"Yes, girls, I'm fine. Everything is alright. Y'all go back to y'all rooms and go to bed."

"Okay, mommy," Annabelle replied.

"Hold up. I know y'all lil' butts aren't going back to bed without giving me smooches."

God heard the girls kissing Billie as he searched Murtaugh's pockets for his car keys. Finding them, he held them up in the air and smiled.

"I love y'all," Billie told the girls.

"We love you too, Billie," Charity said.

God dipped outside, and found two Mustang Cobras parked side by side on the block. He wasn't sure if the white one—or the vintage charcoal gray one—was for Murtaugh. So he pressed the alarm button on the remote of Murtaugh's car keys, then the alarm sounded off the vintage charcoal gray Mustang. He grinned, knowing he'd found the vehicle Murtaugh had driven there. Pulling out his cell phone, he hit up a homeboy of his at a tow yard to come pick it up. While he was waiting for him to come, he removed the ruined front door from off its hinges, and replaced it with the one he had stashed inside of his garage. By the time he was done, the tow truck arrived to take the Mustang Cobra away. God hit his homeboy's hand with five hundred dollars, dapped him up, and he went about his business. Next, he gave Billie a bag of money and told her to give their neighbors on either side of their house five hundred apiece to keep their mouths shut. He knew the police were going to be there shortly, and he wanted to guarantee they wouldn't be ratted out.

"How'd everything go?" God asked, as Billie came through the front door and locked it behind her.

"They agree they weren't going to say anything," Billie informed him. "Yo' neighbor across the street, Gabe, he wouldn't even take the money. He said you're good people and he fucks witchu, and you don't even gotta worry about 'em saying nothing. He's not on that snitch shit. Those were his words."

"That's my nigga," God smiled. "I fuck witcha boy the long way, for real, for real." Billie's face balled up, and she pinched her nose closed, looking at Murtaugh's dead body. "What's wrong?" God frowned, looking back and forth between his wife and the body.

"This nigga starting to stink, babe."

"No shit," God said with a grin. "You used to knock dude's heads off for a living. You should know that after someone dies, they have their last bowel movement."

"Yeah, but I'll never get used to that shit," she replied with a face scrunched with disgust. "Anyway, lemme put this money back up in the safe." She'd just walked passed him when he grabbed her wrist, making her turn around.

"Gemme a kiss, nigga—You know what's up," God told her demandingly. Billie smiled, and they made out like a teenage couple. Grinning, she walked, away wiping the spit at the corner of her mouth. He leaned over the back of the couch and smacked her ass. She chuckled and continued on her way, loving how her man made her feel like she was still in high school.

God smiled and shook his head, as he observed her sauntering away, with her bodacious buttocks rocking from left to right. When he turned back around, the smile dropped from his face as red and blue lights shone on his face through the curtains hanging over the living room's window. He sprung to his feet and peeked through the curtains. As he watched the cops vacate their police car, Billie came from behind him and wrapped her arms around his waist.

"What chu looking at out there, babe?" Billie asked,

with her eyes closed and a grin on her lips.

"These mothafucking faggot-ass cops making their rounds," God answered. "If they come over here, I'm not even gon' bother to answer the door—we got that dead ass cracka on the floor and bullet holes throughout the house. We don't need these pigs snorting around trying to find something to link you and me to this bullshit."

"Agreed."

God and Billie watched the cops until they started to make their way over to their house. Seeing them approaching, they killed the living room lights and sat quietly on the couch, hugged up. The Boys stood outside on their porch, knocking at the door like the typical police. When they didn't get an answer, one of them slid a card into the slight opening of their door. Once Billie had confirmed that they'd pulled off, God snatched the card out the door, read it, tore it up, and tossed the pieces of it in the trash can. When he turned around, Billie was flipping on the light switch. God pulled out his cellular and scrolled through his contacts for a specific number. Billie walked over to him, and looked over his shoulder while holding him around his waist.

"Who are you calling, handsome?" Billie inquired.

"Buck Wild." God looked over his shoulder and kissed her. "I'ma have him and Country get rid of this body," he informed her before placing his cell phone to his ear.

God tried to hit up Buck Wild and Country, but both of their cell phones went to voicemail. He decided he was going to have to get rid of Murtaugh's body himself. He was going to need another car for that. There wasn't any way in hell that he was going to put a dead body in the trunk of his or Billie's whip. Besides, he was sure neither of their vehicle's trunks had enough space to fit Murtaugh's body inside, anyway. With that in mind, God searched through his contacts for a young nigga he was sure could get him any car he desired. The kid went by the name Sticky—on the account of him having sticky fingers (which meant he had a habit of stealing shit). He made his living stealing cars. It was his bread and butter. Although snatching cars was his specialty, Sticky was a man of many trades. This was of utmost necessity because the boy had three baby mamas and twice as many kids to take care of. He hustled coke, drove for Uber, worked as an armed security guard, and hustled niggaz down at the pool hall. On top of that, he cut hair on the side. If it was a dollar to be made, then old Sticky was going to make it.

God tapped the name *Sticky* on his phone's screen, and placed his cellular to his ear, listening to it ring. Sticky picked up on the second ring. God was hitting up his business phone, and he knew if that phone was ringing then the money was calling him.

"Sticky, what up, dog? Yeah, this the God. Look, I needa whip. Matter of fact, I needa 2018 Cadillac XTS, I don't give a fuck what color it is or what it looks like. All I give a fuck about is that it drive like a fucking champ—Unh, huh, how soon can you get it for me?" As he listened to Sticky, he glanced at his timepiece when he'd given him the time he could bring the car by. Now, God had specifically asked for a 2018 Cadillac XTS because it has one of the largest cargo spaces of its class, with eighteen cubic feet of trunk space. "Alright, cool, how much this shit gon' run me? Fa sho', I can fade that. Well, look, write this address down—" he went on to give him the address to his crib. "Smooth. I'll see you once you get here, my nigga. Peace." He disconnected the call. "Yo', the lil' homie said he'll be here in two hours flat. That gives us enough time to clean up this mess and wrap the white boy up in blankets so we can get rid of his body."

"Where are you gonna take it?" Billie inquired curiously, with her hands on her hips and her weight leaning toward one side.

"My uncle works late nights at the mortuary, I can get 'em to cremate the body," God told her. "As a matter of fact, lemme hit this nigga up now to make sure he can do it." He scrolled through the contacts in his cell phone, looking for his homeboy that worked at the mortuary.

"Baby, do you think it's a good idea to talk business like that over a cell phone?"

"Nah, baby, that's why you speak in code," God said, as he listened to the phone ringing. "What's up, unc? Shit, ain't nothing. Say, bruh, my bitch just had puppies, I remember you said your granddaughter wanted one so I was gon' bring 'em by there so you can take a look at 'em. Cool? Okay, I'ma slide through there in, like, three hours, big dog. Alright, peace." He disconnected the call and slid his cell phone into his pocket. "See how easy that was? If he woulda told me that he wasn't cool with seeing the puppies, then that meant I couldn't drop a body on 'em." He pulled off his hoodie and then his wife beater, leaving his muscular physique exposed along with the few tattoos he had. He then told Billie to grab them both a pair of gloves and a few blankets from out of the hallway closet. Once God and Billie cleaned up the mess that was created due to the fight, they wrapped up Murtaugh's dead body so they could dispose of it.

***

Billie sat on the couch, examining her nails and thinking

of how badly she needed to get a manicure. While she was doing this, God was pacing the floor and taking a swig of a Heineken. Sticky was supposed to have been there twenty minutes ago, so he was wondering what the hold-up was. He glanced at his timepiece for the fiftieth time in the past twenty minutes. He ran his hand down his face and blew out his breath, taking another swig of his beer. He pulled out his cell phone to hit up Sticky to see what the fuck was taking him so long, and that was when he heard the doorbell ring. He sat the beer down on the mantle next to the gold urn containing Asad's ashes, and Billie sat up on the couch, looking to the front door. She watched as God looked through the peephole to see who it was. He looked back and told Billie it was Sticky, before opening the front door.

As soon as the door was pulled open, God found himself face to face with Sticky. Sticky was a twenty-year-old kid about five-foot-eleven. He was skinny with a bald peanut head, and a clean-shaven face that made him look younger than he actually was. He had shitty eyesight, so he wore glasses with lenses as thick as the bullet-proof windows at Nix Check Cashing. Sticky was wearing a security guard uniform that was two sizes too big, and black pattern leather boots. God figured he was at work when he'd hit him up about securing the Cadillac, and he'd left to see about snatching it.

"My bad for being late, took a lil' longer than I expected to find the exact one you were looking for," Sticky told him. He shook up his asthma pump and took two puffs of it. He then tossed God the car keys to the Cadillac XTS he'd stolen, and motioned for him to follow him. "Come on, man, its outside."

God went outside with Sticky and checked out the Cadillac. He opened the trunk and took a look inside. It was spacious and definitely had enough room to store Murtaugh's body in. Seeing this, a smile spread across God's face. He cranked it up and drove around the neighborhood for a test drive. The car drove like a fucking dream. He drove back to his crib, and tossed Sticky a bankroll of dead presidents secured by a rubber band. Sticky stuck the bankroll inside of his pocket, shook up with God, and hopped into the car with his baby mama who'd driven him over there.

"Babe, I parked the car in the backyard and left the trunk open," God told Billie, as he walked back inside the house. "I'ma need yo' help dumping this mothafucka inside of the trunk." He slipped the hoodie over his head, and slipped his arms through the sleeves of it. He and Billie strained as they hoisted up Murtaugh's carcass and carried it inside the kitchen. Reaching behind him, God unlocked the back door and pulled it open. He and Billie proceeded out of the door, down the steps, and over to the trunk of the Cadillac. They placed the body inside the trunk and slammed it shut.

God and Billie wiped the sheen of sweat from their foreheads and took a breath. Billie then hugged and kissed him. She looked up into his eyes, as he caressed her cheek with the side of his hand.

"I love you, you know that?" Billie asked him.

"You better, or I'd kick yo' fine ass," God said, with a smirk, causing her to snicker.

"Be careful, please. I cannot stress it enough."

"I will, ma—Try not to worry," God said and kissed her. She held onto his hand for as long as she could, until he walked away. She watched as he jumped in behind the wheel of the Cadillac, cranked it up, and pulled out of the backyard.

"Lord, please, look after my husband, I love 'em entirely too much to lose 'em," Billie said, as she stared up at the lone moon in the sky, with her fingers interlocked. Dropping her hands at her sides, she took a breath and walked back inside the house. Once she was back inside, she closed and locked the door behind her.

***

God made a left at the corner and crossed the threshold onto the grounds of the mortuary. He parked at the rear of the building and hopped out of the Cadillac, slamming the door shut behind him. He took another glance at his digital watch and knocked on the black iron door. Glancing over his shoulder, he impatiently tapped his foot as he waited for the door to be answered. Thirty seconds later, all the iron door's locks were being undone, and it was being pulled open. When the door finally came open, God found Conrad standing before him. At fifty-eight, the old head stood exactly five-foot-nine; five-foot-eleven when he wore boots. He bore a striking resemblance to Billy Dee Williams and even wore his hair like him. He was wearing an ox-blood Nike tracksuit beneath a black apron and Air Force Ones. He sucked on the end of half of a cigar and blew out a cloud of smoke to his left.

Conrad had been slinging dope since the early nineties. He was making so much money he decided to open a business to wash it through. He believed there wasn't any business like the business concerning the handling of a loved one after death. The people that handled funeral arrangements and prepared the dead for burial made some serious dough. Conrad understood that the business he was looking into would never go belly-up. That kind of business was definitely essential because people died every day, and their families had to pay someone to prepare them for their final send-off.

When Conrad was a boy, he worked alongside his grandfather during the summers to earn extra money for back-to-school clothes. His grandfather worked off the books as a mortician for this very wealthy, old white man named Samuel Weinstein. Conrad was just a snot nose kid when he learned the trades of funeral director and mortician, so he knew he could wear both hats. With his mind made up, he went ahead and opened up his very own cemetery. A funeral home, a chapel, mortuary and crematorium—among other tenements—were on the grounds of the premises. In addition to using his business as a place to wash his dirty money through, Conrad also used it as a spot to ship his drugs and stash them. He had the perfect set-up to run both of his businesses; and the best part about it was, no one suspected what he was doing.

There was a rumor spreading around the hood that Conrad was stashing his drugs inside the lining of coffins. Street niggaz had been gossiping about his stash for years, so it was kind of like an urban legend. No one dared to kick in the door of his establishment because it was a well-known fact that Conrad was with the shits. While the so-called streets were afraid to run up in Conrad's spot, there was a little nappy head nigga that didn't give a fuck about making a move against him. He was nine-year-old Kyree Purdy, but in the future the trenches would come to know him as God. God, being the son of two crackheads, didn't have many clothes. In addition, there were a lot of days he didn't have anything to eat. When he'd gotten wind of there being bricks hidden inside the coffins in some OG nigga's funeral home, he made it his business to see about getting his hands on them.

One night, God broke inside of the funeral home and

stole the drugs the streets had been talking about. Conrad caught up with him before he could leave. He had every intention of blowing his brains out, until he discovered he was just a kid. One thing led to another, and they started talking. The OG found out the conditions that God was living under, and his circumstances. Taking pity on him, he took him to grab a bite to eat at a twenty-four-hour Denny's restaurant. They chopped it up over their meals, and God convinced him to let him move drugs for him. With the deal brokered, the young nigga started slinging for Conrad. Soon, he started gaining weight because he was eating. Then, he bought himself clothes, sneakers, underwear, and all of the necessities he needed.

God's parents became suspicious of all the new shit he'd started buying lately. He told them he'd earned the money for everything by cutting lawns every day after school. Although they were crackheads, they weren't stupid. They knew he couldn't have possibly earned all the money he had by mowing a few fucking lawns. They were sure he was doing something illegal, but they didn't know what. One day while God was at school, they snooped around inside of his closet; they found two Adidas sneaker boxes. The first sneaker box had a digital scale, a few straight-back razors, and a sandwich bag of crack rocks. The second sneaker box was loaded with wrinkled dead presidents of all denominations.

God's mother and father tried to exercise the reins of parenthood for the first time in years. When God came back home, they confronted him with the dirty money and the drug paraphernalia they found. He didn't deny his hustling in the streets, and he didn't hold back when he scolded them for being such shitty parents. His mother and father felt like he had to be punished for what he'd done and how he'd come at them. So they kept the money and drugs they'd found in his bedroom, and beat the dog shit out of him. They beat the poor kid to within an inch of his life, and he ended up at children's hospital, inside of the intensive care unit.

Conrad was up there to see him at the hospital every day until he eventually came out of his coma. He got God to tell him who'd assaulted him. The young nigga gave him the raw and uncut truth, which left Conrad in a murderous rage. Conrad murdered his parents and cremated their bodies. When it was time to get God out of the hospital, he was the one to pick him up. He told him his parents had gone missing and no one knew what happened to them. He also told him not to worry about it because he was going to adopt him so he could live with him. God accepted his offer, although he knew in the back of his mind that Conrad had murdered his parents. He didn't give a fuck, though. Whatever feelings he'd had for them were gone after they'd nearly beat him to death.

Conrad raised God into the man he was today. The man was not only a father to him, but he was also his plug. He copped all of his weight for him, and he wouldn't have it any other way. He loved that old nigga as much as he loved Billie and the girls.

"Sup, old man?" God smiled and extended his hand.

"Ain't nothing much, youngsta," Conrad replied, taking the cigar out of his mouth and taking God's hand. They embraced and patted each other on the back. God then pulled out a bankroll secured by a rubber band, and passed it to him. Conrad took it and stashed it inside of his pocket. "I take it the package is inside that Caddy over there." With the hand that held his cigar, Conrad pointed to the Cadillac God had driven there.

"Yes, sir," God answered, as he looked at the Cadillac.

"Alright, junior, let's make this quick." Conrad opened the door all of the way, and put down the stand that would hold it in place. He patted God on his shoulder and motioned for him to follow him to the Cadillac. Once God popped the trunk, he scanned the area to make sure no one was watching them.

"It's all good, son—There isn't anyone here besides you and me," Conrad assured him. Although they'd been doing business with each other for quite some time, God wasn't sure if things had changed around there, so he was just being careful.

"Alright, grab his legs, unc," God said, as he grabbed the upper half of Murtaugh. Conrad grabbed the lower half of him and they carried him off inside of the mortuary.

God and Conrad transported Murtaugh's blanket-wrapped body to the crematorium, and placed it up on the holy metal slab of the retort chamber. Conrad walked over to the gear shaft and turned it up midway. *Froosh!* The blue flames erupted from the isles inside of the retort, startling God who just backed away from it, trying not to get burned.

"Damn! That mothafucka is hot—I can feel the heat from the flames already," God told Conrad, as he stared inside the retort, watching the fire lick away at the air. "Yo', unc, make sure you burn this cracka complete up. I don't want any traces of 'em left behind."

Conrad frowned at God and snatched the cigar out of his mouth, addressing him, "Junior, how long you and I been doing this dance? When I get rid of a nigga, I really get rid of a nigga. I don't leave so much as a goddamn toe nail behind; you should know how I get down. Hell, if my old ass was sloppy, both of our black asses would have been sitting on death row waiting to get the needle."

"I know, unc. I just wanna be sure, is all."

"I got chu faded, youngsta. I'll just crank this bitch up to the max, you feel me? Make sure our friend is gone." Conrad pushed the shaft all the way up, raising the height of the flames inside of the retort.

"See there, that's why I fuck witchu." God smiled and pointed a finger at Conrad. Conrad gave him a curtsey nod and continued to smoke his cigar.

"Go ahead and push 'em in there so we can get this shit over and done with," Conrad told God.

"Right," God replied and began pushing the metal slab into the retort. As he was doing so, he heard a cellular phone vibrating and ringing. Stopping, he looked over to Conrad who was looking at his cell phone. The old man looked up at him and shook his head, letting him know it wasn't his phone. God checked his jack, and it wasn't him either. That's when he looked at Murtaugh's dead body. God's forehead wrinkled curiously, and he quickly un-wrapped the corpse, retrieving the cell phone. Joaquin's name was on the screen of the cellular. Seeing his name made the biggest smile spread across God's lips. He answered the call and brought the cell phone to his ear.

"Yo' man missed, mothafucka!" God disconnected the call and tossed the cellular inside the retort. He then pushed Murtaugh's carcass completely inside the retort, slamming and locking the door securely.

"I got it from here," Conrad assured God, as he placed his hand on his shoulder. When God turned around, he found the old man with his hand held up and open. He shook up with him and embraced him. "I love you, boy."

"I love you too, unc," God told him. "You make sure you hit me if you need anything."

"You do the same," Conrad replied, watching him disappear through the door of the crematorium.

Chapter 3

Joaquin stood out on the tier, rolling himself a fat ass blunt expertly. Taking the blue flame of his lighter, he swept it back and forth across the blunt, sealing it closed. He placed the blunt between his lips, and cupped his hand around it, lighting it up. Joaquin sucked on the end of the blunt, and made the tip of it glow into life. He blew out a cloud of smoke and looked over his budding business. Thinking of what his hard work was doing for him, a smile spread across his face.

Man, shit is really starting to come together for yo' boy. I've had to shed a lot of blood in my lifetime, but that was all to propel someone else into a position of power. Now, the blood I'll shed will be for me to be top dog, Joaquin thought, as he continued to smoke his blunt. He was about to take another drag from it, when he heard a voice at his back.

"Lemme hit that!" Aztec said from behind him. His unannounced presence startled Joaquin and sent him into a coughing fit.

Holding his fist to his mouth, Joaquin looked over his shoulder to see Aztec approaching. The little man was smiling broadly and looking quite amused by his scaring of his street brother.

"Ol' punk-ass, I scared yo' ass, didn't I?" Aztec gave a throaty laugh, doubling over and holding his stomach.

"Whatever, lil' nigga!" Joaquin said, sticking his blunt in his mouth. He slid into a fighter's stance, throwing playful punches and jabs at Aztec. Aztec slid into a fighting stance and started throwing playful punches at him also. They danced around the top tier, laughing and horsing around like blood brothers do.

Having grown tired of playing, Joaquin stopped and

took his blunt from out of his mouth. He dumped some of its grayish black ashes from the tip of it and embraced Aztec with a one-armed hug.

"On some real shit, lemme hit that though, bro," Aztec said seriously and extended his hand for the blunt, which Joaquin passed to him.

"Yo, you took care of that business for me, right?" Joaquin inquired about the task he'd assigned to him.

Aztec nodded and blew out smoke. "Yeah, I took care of it."

"That's why you're my nigga, Tec. You stay on yo' shit."

"I gots to, I'm your soldado."

Joaquin nodded understandingly and said, "Where Hugo and Murtaugh?"

"I just got off the teléfono with Murtaugh, said he's indisposed—whatever the fuck that shit means. Here." Aztec passed the blunt back to Joaquin. He watched, as the man he looked up to as a big brother looked over his facility proudly. Joaquin looked like a king looking over his kingdom.

"Why are you smiling like a pedophile at a four-year-old boy's birthday party?"

"One day I'm gonna run this world, Tec!" Joaquin swore as he dumped the ashes from his blunt and took a pull from it. "Today it will be the city, but tomorrow—tomorrow it will be the entire goddamn world. And that's on my granny's daughter." He continued to take in the fruits of his labor from where he stood out on the tier, admiring everyone and everything in it.

"You've got all of this coke, so now what?" Aztec said, shrugging. "You plan on being Scarface or something?"

"You've always thought too small, baby boy," Joaquin told him. "Fuck Scarface, my nigga, I'ma be Sosa!"

Aztec nodded understandingly and said, "Street dreams."

Joaquin hung his arm around Aztec's neck and looked down, taking pulls from his blunt and blowing smoke into the air.

"Nah, not any more, lil' bro. Tomas helped me turn that dream into a reality." Joaquin smiled. "This is a five-million-dollar underground crack manufacturing lab. This right here is an engineering masterpiece, my nigga. Its right underneath a one hundred unit apartment complex, and it's equipped with a state-of-the-art filtration system to evacuate toxic fumes; it's also capable of cooking between one hundred to three hundred pounds of cocaine a week."

Aztec leaned over the guardrail to get a closer look at the operation below. "Damn, this is—this is the most beautiful thing I've ever seen."

Below the tier there was a super lab where machine gun toting goons walked around, keeping an eye on things. All of the crackheads Murtaugh and Hugo had kidnapped were working to produce crack cocaine. The fiends—male and female—were topless, wearing only a head covering, latex gloves and an apron. They all wore a tracking device collar around their neck. The small black box attached to it had a blue light on it, which let any observer know it was functioning and its wearer wasn't out of bounds. The tracking device also acted as a shock collar, and would explode if you tampered with it.

On the main floor, inside the room on the left, there were fiends cutting crack into five-dollar, ten-dollar and twenty-dollar sized rocks. Inside the room on the right side of the main floor, there were fiends bagging up the rocks. Once the merchandise was finished being packaged, it was loaded into the back of vans. The product was then driven to specific locations where it would be distributed out of a crack house, or slung on the corners by D-boys. At the end of every business week, *The Collectors* would be sent out to pick up the profits from the drug sales, which would then be driven out to a well-guarded count house. Later, the dirty money would be deposited into different bank accounts overseas that the federal government couldn't fuck with.

Ms. Jones stood in the room alongside other crackheads chopping up rocks to be bagged. The old head looked the same save for her hideously scarred back she'd gotten on account of Aztec whipping her mercilessly. She'd refused to give up her recipe for cooking the illegal substance that the streets loved, so it was up to little gangsta to break her. To her credit, she didn't give up the ingredients until he'd threatened to rape Charity right before he slit her throat.

Ms. Jones was willing to call his bluff, until she saw the seriousness in his eyes and the sadistic smile on his face. There wasn't any doubt in her mind that he'd go through with his threat, so she told him what he wanted to know. She was then forced to show the other crackheads how to cook the product like she did. Afterwards, she rotated between the assignments all of them were given inside the lab.

Ms. Jones' eyes shifted around the room to see if the guards were watching her as she chopped off a dime-sized rock. She balled the rock inside her fist and pretended to be cutting more. Once she saw that the guards were paying attention to her, she swiftly tossed the rock inside her mouth and swallowed it. She had plans of passing the rock on through a bowel movement later and smoking it. Ms. Jones went to chop another rock with the Gemstar razor, and the stock of a machine gun slammed into the side of her head. She winced as the side of her head ricocheted off the ground. Slowly, she turned over on her back, seeing double of one guard standing over her with his machine gun. By the menacing look on his face, she could tell he was pissed.

"You think I didn't see that, whore? Spit it out! Go on, spit it out! Or, so help me—I'll carve it outta your belly." The guard switched gloved hands with his machine gun and pulled out a bowie knife. His hostile eyes bored into Ms. Jones as he slowly approached her. A terrified look was on her face as she backed up into the corner of the room, on the palms of her hands and the balls of her feet.

The other crackheads continued to chop up the drugs, while nosily paying attention to what the guard was about to do to Ms. Jones. Though some of them wanted to help her, none of them was foolish enough to make a move. They were too fearful of being dealt the same fate as her.

"You've got 'til the count of five." The guard warned her and started counting down. "One—"

Ms. Jones got down on her hands and knees toward the guard. She stuck two fingers as far inside of her mouth as she could, trying to make herself throw up the crack rock she'd swallowed. She gagged and coughed, as tears streamed down her cheeks. A river of murky saliva with food particles in it spilled out of her mouth and splashed on the floor. Ms. Jones looked back and forth between the approaching guard and what she was vomiting.

"Two, three—" the guard continued to count down. He clutched the bowie knife in his hand firmly and prepared to strike Ms. Jones, if she didn't present him with the crack she'd swallowed.

A couple of the crackheads shook their head in pity for her, while others crossed themselves in the sign of the crucifix.

"Four, five—Time's up!" the guard said and snatched Ms. Jones up by the front of her apron, pinning her to the wall. He wrapped his hand tightly around her neck, causing her to hold onto his wrist. She made an ugly face as she tried to loosen his hand from around her throat, which was stopping her from getting oxygen.

The guard cocked the hand back that clutched the bowie knife. He was on the verge of stabbing Ms. Jones so he could open up her stomach and get the rock she'd swallowed. She squeezed her eyelids shut and whispered a prayer to Almighty God to save her life.

"O most merciful Jesus, with a contrite heart and penitent spirit, I bow down in profound humility before your divine majesty. I adore you as my supreme Lord and Master. I believe in you, I hope in—" Ms. Jones cut her thoughts short, believing she should have been gutted by now. Surprised to have still been alive, she opened her eyes and was surprised to see Joaquin holding the guard by his wrist.

"What seems to be the problem here?" Joaquin asked, as he took the bowie knife from the guard's gloved hand.

"This smoked-out-ass bitch took a rock off the table and swallowed it." The guard gave him a report. "I guess she planned on throwing it back up later to smoke it."

Joaquin's head snapped in her direction. He looked like he was pissed off. Seeing how angry he was made Ms. Jones fearful of him, and she swallowed the nervous lump in her throat. Her forehead was covered in beads of sweat. One of the beads slid down and dripped off the corner of her brow, splashing on the floor below.

"Is that true?" Joaquin asked. When she didn't say anything, he stepped closer to her. "I'm not gonna ask again." She nodded rapidly, and hoped he didn't allow the guard to carve open her belly.

Joaquin took a deep breath and ran his hand down his face. He tucked one hand under his arm and tapped the bowie knife against his cheek as he thought on the situation. Coming to a conclusion, he grabbed three crack rocks off the table top and told the guard to let Ms. Jones go. The guard looked at him like he was mad, and he tilted his head to the side. Joaquin looked at him, like, *Nigga, don't challenge me.* The guard took a deep breath and looked at Ms. Jones, slowly releasing her neck from his grip. She grimaced as she massaged her neck. She watched as Joaquin flipped the bowie knife over so he'd be holding its blade in his hand and passed it to the guard. The guard sheathed the knife and walked away. Joaquin patted him on his back as he went about his business patrolling the facility. Once he had gone, Joaquin turned his attention back to Ms. Jones.

"Are you, okay?" Joaquin asked her, as he placed his hand on her shoulder. He was holding her gaze as he spoke to her.

"Yes—yes—thank you," Ms. Jones said, still rubbing her neck.

"Good, good," Joaquin replied, taking her hand and placing the three crack rocks inside of her palm. She looked down at what he had put in her palm and smiled. Right after, he mad-dogged her and balled up her palm, closing it into a fist. He squeezed her fist around the rocks to tight that they both could literally hear the bones in her fingers cracking. She winced in pain, hoping he'd show mercy and leave her with the usage of her hand. She jumped when he jabbed his finger into her face, wagging it as he talked to her sternly. "Enjoy that high while you can. Right now, I'm letting you breeze with that lil' stunt you pulled 'cause I'm in a good mood, but should you ever—and I do mean ever—steal from me again, I swear upon Jesus and his twelve apostles, I'll carve your fucking eyeballs out of your head. Do you understand?" he asked, breathing his hot breath in her face.

"Yes—yes, I—I understand—And it will never happen again," Ms. Jones promised with teary eyes as she shook uncontrollably. She was so terrified that her teeth began to chatter. Feeling teardrops sliding down her face, she wiped them away with her curled finger.

"Great," Joaquin said with a smile. He fixed her hair and straightened out her clothing and apron. He then caressed her cheek with the side of his hand. Abruptly, his face morphed into a mask of hatred, making him look demonic. "Now, get cho ass back to work." He flashed a smile at her again, and smacked her on her ass before heading out of the room.

Ms. Jones went back to work at the table, chopping up the rocks and occasionally wiping away the teardrops that fell from her eyes.

Joaquin took out his cellular and hit Murtaugh up again. Murtaugh's phone rang, and as the line went through, Joaquin spoke. "You took care of that for me?" he asked, as he emerged from out of the door of the room the crackheads were chopping up the product in. The person at the other end of the line, who he knew was God—by his voice—basically told him that Murtaugh was dead. Shortly thereafter, he heard the cell phone being thrown into something, and then it disconnected. Frowning, Joaquin looked at his cellular like there were cockroaches crawling on it. He then placed it back inside of his pocket. The response he'd gotten from God let him know that Murtaugh was dead. "Fuck! Goddamn it!" he raged, walking by a window, punching it. He then kicked over a nearby metal push cart, and it crashed to the floor.

"Yo, what's up, big bro?" Aztec asked, concerned, from the tier, with his arms spread wide open.

***

Buck Wild pulled up outside the location that Hugo had unwillingly given him, and turned his whip off. He and Country slipped on their gloves and put on neoprene masks that covered the lower half of their face. They pulled the drawstrings of their hoods, and enclosed them around their heads before tying them up. Afterwards, Buck Wild pulled his Tec-9 from underneath his seat and made sure it was cocked, locked and ready.

Hearing his cell phone ring, Country held up his finger for Buck Wild to give him a minute. When he saw it was his baby mama calling him, he rolled his eyes and blew his breath, annoyed.

"Man, I don't feel like hearing this bitch mouth right now, bruh. Fuck!" Country complained as he held his cell phone.

"Who's that?" Buck Wild asked curiously.

"My punk-ass B.M., dog," Country answered him, looking down at the cellular's screen. It suddenly stopped ringing.

"Man, just holla at her once we finish handling this business. Shit not gon' take that long. We're just gon' run up in here, crush this nigga and smash out. Look, it stopped ringing anyway. Come on."

Country's cell started right back up, ringing again.

"See there, dog, here Nadine ass goes again. Lemme answer this shit. She just had my shawty, maybe something is up with 'em."

"Man, make it quick so we can squash this fool," Buck Wild said, annoyed. Country's baby mama had always been a pain in the ass, but she seemed to have gotten worse since she had his baby. With all the tricks Nadine had his cousin doing, and all the burning hoops she had him jumping through, Buck Wild made up his mind to never have children of his own. As a matter of fact, he was going to set up an appointment with his PCP as soon as possible, to see about getting a vasectomy. Fuck that shit!

Buck Wild listened to his cousin go back and forth with his baby mama for the next five minutes, before he started rushing him off the phone. They exchanged 'I love yous', and Country disconnected the call, smiling.

"I can't believe this shit. A goddamn lovesick killa. I've done seen it all." Buck Wild shook his head and ran his hand down his face.

"Fuck you mean, bruh? That's my shawty, the mother of my child."

"Nigga, y'all got one toxic ass relationship," Buck Wild told him, straight up. "All y'all do is argue, fight, and fuck! Make up—just to do the shit all over again."

"Relationships aren't perfect, dog. You'd know that if you didn't spend yo' time running up in hoes every chance you got instead of tryna find you something real." Country slipped his ski-mask over his head and adjusted the eye holes of it.

Buck Wild pulled his ski-mask over his head and turned to address Country. "Man, shut cho big, dumb country ass up and get the fuck outta this car so we can kill this nigga."

Buck Wild and Country hopped out of the car, slamming their doors shut behind them. Buck Wild popped the trunk, and Country pulled out a black pistol-grip shotgun. He racked the shotgun and slammed the trunk shut.

"Nigga murdered and butchered the young homie Asad, and then had fools smoke his baby mama—Oh, yeah, nigga fa sho' getting dealt with," Buck Wild said, as he and Country jogged toward their destination.

"Fucking right, we're doing this shit for our young jit

Asad," Country told Buck Wild while extending his gloved fist toward him.

"For Asad," Buck Wild agreed and touched fists with Country.

Joaquin was a dead man!

Buck Wild and Country invaded the front yard of Joaquin's house, like a military trained unit. They made their way upon the front porch, making note of the lights being out. They posted up on either side of the door. Buck Wild looked at Country, and gave him the signal to pick the lock. As Country went about the task, Buck Wild clutched his Tec-9 with both hands, watching his back. Having picked the lock, Country opened the black iron screen door and took a step back, holding his shotgun with both hands. Buck Wild stepped up, telling Country he was going to kick in the door on the count of three. Country nodded.

Buck Wild took a stance and took a breath, preparing to kick the door in. Inside of his head he counted down from three.

Boom! Boom! Buck Wild kicked the door twice with all of his might. The second try made the door fly inward and sprayed splinters everywhere. Buck Wild and Country rushed inside of the living room, ready to lay down anyone that posed a threat to them. Seeing the living room was clear, they started to check out the rest of the house, and the lights came on. Startled, Buck Wild and Country looked around confusingly. The front door slammed shut hard and locked.

Buck Wild and Country whipped around to it, wondering how the fuck it closed when there wasn't anyone there. Country ran over to the front door, twisting its knob back and forth, but it wouldn't open. He tried to kick it open like Buck Wild had, but it still wouldn't budge.

"Fuck you doing, man? Kick that bitch open!" Buck

Wild told him, as he rushed over in his direction.

"I tried to, mothafucka, but it's not budging!" Country said angrily, and punched the door.

"Stand back!" Buck Wild said and nudged him aside. He tried to kick the door open like he had before, but all he ended up doing was injuring his ankle. "Aaaah, damn it!" He grimaced and grabbed for his aching ankle.

"You all right?" Country asked, concerned, resting his hand on his cousin's shoulder.

"Man, hell no, I think I fractured my shit! Sssssss!" Buck Wild sucked his teeth in pain.

Suddenly, the 50-inch flat screen mounted to the wall powered on, and Joaquin's face filled the monitor.

"If you're seeing my face now, that means you've broken into my shit and you know what that means—" Joaquin said, drawing Buck Wild and Country's attention. They looked to monitor, shocked to see his face. They exchanged glances and looked back up at the flat screen. "That's ya ass!" Joaquin threw his head back and laughed maniacally.

"Woof, woof, woof, woof, woof!"

"Woof, woof, woof, woof, woof!"

The vicious barks of hostile hounds filled the air from somewhere deep down inside of the house. Buck Wild and Country whipped around to the kitchen, to see the basement door swing open. They could hear the dogs hurrying up the basement's staircase as fast as they could. Their barking grew louder and louder, the closer they came to the surface above.

The flat screen powered off, and its monitor went black.

"Oooh, shit!" Buck Wild and Country said in unison upon hearing the dogs.

"Woof, woof, woof, woof, woof!"

"Woof, woof, woof, woof, woof!"

Two big ass Rottweilers emerged from the basement, and charged at Buck Wild and Country. Their evil red eyes and saliva-dripping fangs made them look like the lap dogs of Satan. Buck Wild pointed his Tec-9 at one of the beasts and pulled its trigger. A quick burst of fire spat out of the semi-automatic weapon before it jammed. When Buck Wild tried to un-jam it, the Rottweiler latched onto his sleeve of his jacket and shook its head from left to right, growling.

Bloom!

Country's shotgun recoiled as it fired at the Rottweiler, looking to chew him a new asshole. The dog yelped and whimpered, having been peppered with buck shots. Being wounded didn't stop the wicked beast from trying to attack Country again. Before the Rottweiler could sink its razor-sharp teeth into Country, he aimed his shotgun at it again and fired—twice more! The Rottweiler howled in pain and ran around the living room, knocking over the coffee table, a vase and a lamp. It then slumped in the corner, whimpering and bleeding before it eventually died.

"Aaaaah, shit! Get this mothafucka off me, man! Shoot 'em! Shoot this goddamn dog!" Buck Wild called out to Country, as he spun the remaining Rottweiler around the living room. He punched and kicked it several times, but it wouldn't turn him loose. It had a lock on him that had to be pried off with a crowbar.

"I'm trying, bruh! You gotta hold still so I can getta clear shot!" Country said, as he continuously tried to draw a bead on the beast to no avail. "Fuck it!" he switched hands with the shotgun and drew his bowie knife, stalking over to the wild dog. He curled his knife underneath the Rottweiler's jugular and yanked it around. Instantly, blood sprayed out of the beast's neck, and it released Buck Wild. It harped and gagged as blood gushed out of its wound. The hound staggered around the living room like it was drunk, before collapsing. The animal laid lifelessly on the floor, eyes wide and tongue hanging out of his mouth. A pool of blood quickly formed around it.

Buck Wild's chest heaved up and down. He un-jammed his Tec-9 and spat fire at the Rottweiler's corpse, blowing its skull and chest apart. Two flies swarmed around the dog's mutilated head for a moment before landing on it, rubbing its limbs together.

"Mothafucka!" Buck Wild spat on the Rottweiler's carcass.

"You good, bruh?" Country asked him.

"Yeah, I'm straight—Let's get the fuck outta here!" Buck Wild said. He tucked his Tec-9 and hoisted up a chair at the dining room table. He ran at the large window of the living room, and hurled the chair at it with all of his might. The chair deflected off of the window and tumbled across the floor. "What the fuck is up?" he asked Country, as he pulled out his Tec-9 again. Country shrugged. "Blast it, my nigga!"

Together, Buck Wild and Country unloaded on the window, causing the curtains hanging over it to ruffle as they were shredded. Buck Wild frowned, seeing that their ammunition didn't have any effect on the window's glass. Country walked over to the window and saw scratches on it from them shooting it. His forehead creased with lines behind the ski-mask, as he knocked on it. The glass was solid.

"This shit is bullet-proof, dog—Ain't no way we getting through this bitch!" Country told him.

"Maybe not through these windows, but that front door—" Buck Wild pointed his Tec-9 at the front door they'd come through earlier. "That motha is wood, and I'm blasting right through it!" He ran over to the front door and lifted up his Tec-9. He was about to pull its trigger when he heard hissing all around the living room. He and Country exchanged glances, wondering what was happening. Country shrugged. Right then, metal bars slid across the front door and down across the windows. Buck Wild darted inside the kitchen. Metal bars went across the back door, and down across the window above the kitchen sink. "What the fuck, man?"

Buck Wild threw down his Tec-9 and ran over to the back door. He stepped upon the metal bars and grabbed hold of the ones at the center of the door. Grunting, he pulled and tugged on them, trying to yank them free from across the door.

"Son of a bitch!" Buck Wild yelled and kicked the metal bars in frustration. He turned around to find Country sitting his shotgun down on the counter top and climbing upon the kitchen sink. He pulled and tugged on the metal bars like Buck Wild had, but they weren't coming loose. "Hey, dumbass, I already tried that!"

"Aye, suck my dick, alright?" Country said hostilely, grabbing the bulge in his jeans. "I'm not in the mood to hear all of yo' pissing and moaning. We needa try to get the fuck outta here before them Boys (the police) show—"

Country cut himself short, hearing spraying sounds coming from the living room, dining room and the kitchen. Country and Buck Wild did a three hundred-and-sixty-degree turn where they were standing at the center of the kitchen floor. They saw short metal barrels spraying a green gas which was quickly filling up the house, making it cloudy. They started gagging and coughing so much that they pulled off their ski-masks. They narrowed their eyelids and tried to hold their breaths, but they could only do it for so long.

"What the fuck is this shit? Poison?" Country asked, gagging and coughing.

"Nah, nah, it's—it's—it's—sleeping gas. I can—I can—feel my—self—getting, uhhh—" Buck Wild's eyes rolled to their whites, and he collapsed to the floor. He lay there, knocked out cold.

"Buck! Buck! Nigga, wake up! Wake up!" Country called out to his cousin as he tried to shake him awake, but he was fast asleep. Country, feeling woozy, staggered over to the back door and started kicking at the metal bars. When that didn't work, he hoisted up his shotgun and blasted at the metal bars. *Click, click, click, click!* "Fuck!" Country turned the shotgun over in his hands and cocked it over his shoulder. Using it as a baseball bat, he swung it against the metal bars again and again, bending it at a funny angle. He swung the shotgun again at the metal bars, but he suddenly dropped it. His eyes rolled to their whites and he made an—*uhhh!*—before collapsing to the floor, knocked out.

As soon as Country had passed out, the short metal barrels drew back into the corners of their respective rooms, and the ventilation systems opened. Slowly, the green fog that had consumed all of the rooms seeped out of the vents, leaving the house completely clear.

Chapter 4

The metal bars drew back from across the front door, the back door, and from over all of the windows. A second later, the front door clicked and swung open. Joaquin and Aztec walked inside, holding guns at their sides and looking around the house. Joaquin had the security system linked to his cell phone so he'd know when someone had broken inside his house. As soon as he'd gotten the notification that the sanctity of his home had been breached, he and Aztec broke hell of speeding laws getting to his crib.

Joaquin spotted Country lying out inside the kitchen. He nudged Aztec and pointed to them. Cautiously, they moved into the kitchen. Once they saw both Country and Buck Wild asleep from the gas, tension released from their bodies. They tucked their guns. Aztec kicked Buck Wild's sneaker to see if he'd move, but he didn't. The nigga farted! Aztec frowned and turned his head, pulling his shirt up over his nose.

"Funky-ass nigga!" Aztec said, and kicked Buck Wild in his side. "What're you doing?" he asked Joaquin, seeing him take something from underneath the kitchen sink. When Joaquin turned around, he was holding something black and shaped like a rectangle. Aztec thought it was an electric shaver until Joaquin squeezed the sides of it, causing electricity to bounce back and forth between its antennas. It was a stun gun.

"I was just getting my toy so we can play with our new friends." Joaquin smiled devilishly and triggered the stun gun. It buzzed and made a zapping sound, bouncing electricity between its antennas. Aztec smiled and held out his hands for Joaquin to toss the stun gun to him. As soon as Joaquin tossed the stun gun over to him, Aztec held it up and triggered it, watching the electricity bounce back and forth between its antennas.

"You hear that, fellas? We're about to have some fun." Aztec smiled devilishly, as he looked from Country to Buck Wild.

"Help me get these two dumbasses down inside of the basement," Joaquin told Aztec, as he pushed Buck Wild over on his back. He then grabbed him by his ankles, grunting as he dragged him toward the basement. He became hot and sweaty from dragging him across the kitchen floor. Although Buck Wild didn't weigh that much, he was technically dead weight.

Joaquin dragged Buck Wild over to the basement door and pushed him down the staircase. He tumbled a quarter of the way down.

"Aye, I'ma—I'ma need some help with this big one! This sucka is heavy!" Aztec said over his shoulder, holding both of Country's ankles. His face was sweaty and hot. "I'ma fuck around and give myself a hernia tryna drag his big ass."

Joaquin wiped the beads of sweat from his forehead and walked over to Aztec. He grabbed one of Country's ankles while Aztec held the other. Together, they grimaced as they dragged him across the kitchen floor over to the basement door and placed him on the staircase. Winded, Aztec wiped his sweaty face with the lower half of his shirt and hunched over, with his hands on his knees. He breathed heavily, chest heaving up and down.

"Man, what the fuck do they feed them big country mothafuckaz down south?" Aztec inquired.

"I don't know. But when you find out, be sure to tell me so we'll both know." Joaquin wiped his sweaty forehead with the back of his hand. He then pressed a button on the side of the basement door which instantly converted the staircase into a ramp. Country and Buck Wild slid down the ramp and across the basement floor, bumping up against the washer and dryer down there. Although Joaquin couldn't see that they'd bumped against the two white machines, he could tell by the sound they made that they had made contact with them. He flipped on a red switch above the button he'd pressed that converted the staircase. The basement lit up. Country and Buck Wild were lying side by side against the washer and dryer. Once Joaquin pressed the button again, the staircase transformed back into its original form.

Recalling something, Joaquin snapped his fingers and darted back inside of the kitchen. He returned with a worn copper brown leather bag. He unzipped it and pulled out handcuffs by his pinky finger. He smiled wickedly at Aztec and let the handcuffs drop back inside of the bag. He patted Aztec on the shoulder and motioned for him to follow him, as he began his descent down the staircase. Aztec closed and locked the basement door behind him, following behind Joaquin. He smiled wickedly as well, rubbing his hands together, thinking about torturing Buck Wild and Country.

***

Handcuffed, Buck Wild and Country hung from a pipe in the ceiling of the basement, ankles chained down by one hundred pound weights. They were butt naked, dicks hanging from their nappy nest of pubic hairs. They were soaking wet, dripping water onto the cold concrete floor. For the better part of an hour, Aztec had been shocking them with the stun gun and trying to get them to give up the whereabouts of God. Every time the water appeared to be drying up on the cousins, Aztec would splash them with a bucket of water and electrocute their asses again. Joaquin played the sideline in a chair, watching the show while taking the occasional swig of his Corona.

Although the pain from being electrocuted was unbearable, Buck Wild and Country were holding strong and refusing to give up God's location. Joaquin had to salute their gangsta. He knew lesser men would have given up their comrade by now, but not these two. He was sure in time he'd know what he needed to know, though. Being one of the top enforcers of his father's cartel back in Mexico, he'd put the most stalwart of soldiers of rival cartels through medieval times' throes of torture, and they eventually told him what he wanted to know. Though he was hoping not to take it to those extreme measures with Buck Wild and Country, he was definitely prepared to.

"You ready to start talking now, homie?" Aztec asked Country after shocking him with the stun gun. He was wearing a black leather apron, yellow dishwashing gloves and black rubber boots.

Country's eyelids were narrowed into slits, and he was breathing heavily, his chest heaving up and down. Beads of water slid down his face and hairy chest, dripping on the floor.

"Okay—okay, I'll tell you—I'll tell you—" Country said in defeat. He couldn't take much more of the torture. Hearing him say this, Aztec smiled triumphantly and looked back at Joaquin who smirked at him, giving him the thumbs up. He turned back to Country who spat a gooey yellowish loogie in his face. Mad-dogging him, he said, "Suck my big black dick, you wetback son of a bitch!"

Aztec looked to Joaquin who was laughing and smacking his knee.

"Yo—yo, I know you're not gonna let homeboy talk to you like that? I just know you're not!" Joaquin said, as he continued to laugh.

Aztec frowned and wiped the loogie from his face with his yellow dishwashing gloved hand. He stepped to Country, grinning sinisterly. Clutching him by his neck, he pressed the stun gun against his wet genitals and squeezed its trigger, sending 50,000 volts through his lower region. Country threw his head back and screamed in excruciation, showcasing all the gold teeth in his mouth. Aztec took the stun gun from his balls and fired on his mouth, bloodying it. Country's eyes rolled around in his head dizzily. He harped up the blood in a loogie and spat it on the floor.

"Oh, you musta thought I forgot about chu, huh? Yo' ass getting it too!" Aztec told Buck Wild before he electrocuted his dick and balls like he had done Country.

"Graaaaaahhh!" Buck Wild threw his head back and hollered in agony.

Aztec snatched his stun gun away from Buck Wild's genitals. He kicked him in the stomach and punched him in the jaw, sending water and blood flying.

"Okay, let's move along to the second method of torture," Aztec said, as he sat the stun gun aside on a nearby stack of cardboard boxes. He pulled out a handgun with a silencer on it and aimed it at Country's right kneecap. He was about to pull its trigger when he heard a cell phone ringing. He and Joaquin's forehead deepened with creases. Joaquin held up a finger for him to wait a minute. He searched the piles of clothing on the floor and found a cellular phone in the pocket of Country's jeans. After pulling out the cell phone, Joaquin looked at its display. *Baby Mama* was on it. He tossed the cell phone over to Aztec. He looked at the screen and then showed it to Country. "What else we got over there, big bro?" he asked Joaquin, but he was looking at Country. He appeared to be alert, having seen his baby mama calling him.

Joaquin walked toward Aztec and Country, looking through the wallet he'd found in his jeans. Finding something he thought was interesting, he pulled it out and dropped the wallet on the floor. He had Country's driver's license and a picture of him, his baby mama and their daughter. Joaquin showed the pictures and the license to Aztec who smiled. He took the license and picture, showing them up to Country for him to see.

"Beautiful familia you got here, dog," Aztec said to him by way of a compliment. "You know, it would be a shame if something were to happen to 'em."

Country scowled, and his nostrils flared. His eyes seemed to have turned red from rage. He bucked on the pipe, as he tried to get loose and beat Aztec's ass.

"You punk-ass mothafucka, if you go near my fucking family I'll kill yo' ass, you hear me? I'll fucking kill you, bitch!" Country screamed loud, making spit fly from his lips.

"I swear before Almighty God, I'll murder everyone you love if you touch my niece, nigga! You violated by bringing my fam into this! You're living on borrowed time, homeboy, borrowed time!" Buck Wild screamed hatefully, as he bucked on the pipe as well. He tried his damndest to get free, but his efforts were in vain.

"Shut the fuck up!" Joaquin spat heatedly, as he backhand-punched Buck Wild and busted his mouth. The blow silenced him, and he spat blood on the floor. "You niggaz have gotten beside yourselves, talking all of this rah, rah shit while you hanging from the fucking ceiling. I don't wanna hear notta 'nother word from you bitchez!" He looked at Aztec. "Tec, shoot to this nigga's crib; get his B.M. and his shorty and bring 'em back here now! We're no longer tryna find out where this nigga God is hiding, we're now orchestrating a hit."

"Now, we're talking." Aztec smiled and dapped up Joaquin. He removed the black leather apron from over his head and pulled off the yellow dishwashing gloves. After he tucked his gun at the small of his back, he patted Joaquin on his shoulder and told him he'd be right back. Country mad-dogged Aztec as he headed up the staircase, but he didn't say a word for fear of retaliation.

Joaquin walked over to Country, cracking the knuckles of both of his hands. Hearing him approaching, Country looked his way, wondering what he had in mind to do to him. Joaquin stopped before him, giving him two body shots and a haymaker across his chin, knocking him out cold. Country's head hung, and blood spewed from out of his mouth, spilling to the floor.

"Might notta said nothing, but I know what cho ass was thinking," Joaquin said as he walked away, wiping his bloody knuckles with a red bandana.

I coulda called Annabelle and got her to tell me their whereabouts, but I don't wanna risk her cell phone ringing and Billie or God finding out she has it. This new plan I have in mind will yield the results I want. And on top of that I won't even have to get my hands dirty.

Aztec came down the staircase with Nadine held at gunpoint. She was crying her eyes out with her son strapped to her chest.

"Oh, my god, Atticus—what have you done to 'em? What have you done to my fiancé?" Nadine cried and whimpered, smacking her hand over her nose and mouth. The icy platinum engagement ring on her finger twinkled with the light reflected off it.

"We beat the shit outta him and electrocuted 'em—But no need to be crying and shit, he's still alive," Joaquin told her as he lugged a big bucket of water over to where she was. "You may wanna stand back, 'less you don't mind this water splashing on you," he told Nadine, and she took a step back. He turned to Country and splashed him with the bucket of water. Country threw his head back and gasped for air, looking around like he didn't know where he was. When his eyes landed on Nadine and his baby, he became concerned. Thoughts of all the terrible things Aztec and Joaquin had in store for them went through his mind. Right then he became fearful for them. He could accept whatever those two wild ass Mexicans niggaz did to him. But he couldn't live with himself if they were to harm his family.

"Baby, are you alright? Did they hurt chu?" Country asked her, as beads of water slid down his face and dripped off his chin.

"No, baby, I'm fine—We're fine," Nadine assured him, as she caressed the side of his face, looking up into his eyes.

"For now—" Aztec warned.

"What the fuck is that 'pose to mean?" Country asked, gritting his teeth.

Joaquin blocked Country's sight of Aztec by stepping in front of him. "It means, if you don't cooperate with us then there's no telling what—" he yanked Nadine's head back by her individual braids, causing her to yelp and her baby to cry aloud "—May happen to your lil' family." Keeping his eyes on Country, Joaquin licked Nadine from the bottom of her chin and up the side of her face. "If you know what I mean." Joaquin implied that they'd rape Nadine, but that wasn't his forte. He didn't get down like that. He was just fucking with Country. But make no mistake, the man was most definitely a killa, and he didn't have any problems with bodying a bitch.

"You mothafucka, I'll—Aaaaaah!" Country threw his

head back, hollering in pain as Aztec electrocuted him with the stun gun.

"Leave 'em alone, mothafucka!" Buck Wild growled in a rage. It was killing him not to be able to put hands on Aztec for what he was doing to his cousin.

"Hazme, chupapollas! (*Make me, cocksucka!*)"Aztec told Buck Wild, as he continued to electrocute a helpless Country.

"Stop, stop, please, stop!" Nadine pleaded with Aztec. The baby cried louder and louder. She bounced him up and down, trying to hush him up.

Joaquin gave Aztec the signal for him to stop his torturing of Country. Aztec took the stun gun from Country's side, and kicked him in his hairy wet buttocks, causing him to swing slightly from the pipe.

"He's—he's hungry—I've gotta—I've gotta feed 'em." Nadine stammered to Joaquin. He gave her a nod, letting her know it was okay for her to breastfeed her child. She walked off to the side, unstrapped the baby from his carrier, and pulled out her right breast. She brought her thick nipple toward the baby's mouth, and he quickly latched onto it, sucking on it hungrily. He quieted down, and she comforted him, patting his back soothingly. She slipped down his fine hair, and kissed him on the top of his head. "That's all it was, huh? You were just hungry, huh, man? Momma's baby was just hungry." She kissed the top of his head again, and continued to stroke his fine hair down.

"You're in no position to be threatening us, big man—In fact, you're at our mercy, check this out," Joaquin said, as he approached Country. Stopping in front of him, he looked up into his eyes. "I no longer want to know yo' bitch-ass boss's whereabouts so I can blow his face off. Nahhh, see, instead, I want you and yo' man here to track God down and bring 'em to me. I'll have my hittas do the rest." Joaquin looked deadly serious as he said those words. Country started to say something, but Joaquin held up his hand, stopping him. "The only thing I wanna hear out of your mouth is '*Yes, me and my nigga are gonna handle that*'. Otherwise, I'ma have my young bull here putta cap in yo' baby mama's head and then in yo' lil' nigga's head after that." He hung his arm around Aztec's neck and pulled him close. "Go on. Tell me what I wanna hear."

Country shut his eyelids briefly and took a breath. He hated he had to submit to Joaquin, but he didn't have any choice. He and his family's lives were on the line. "Yes, me and my nigga are gonna handle that," he reluctantly stated, defeat dripping from his vocal cords.

"Good. Very good." Joaquin smirked and patted Country on his cheek. He then leaned forward and whispered into his ear. "Keep in mind, if you don't make that drop to my men, you're gonna be making funeral arrangements for yo' bitch and yo' son. Understand?" he asked with seriousness bleeding from his eyes.

Country looked over at Nadine breastfeeding his baby. He could tell that she was petrified. He was mad at himself for putting him and his family in this position. He knew that his only way out of this mess was to comply with what Joaquin wanted. Otherwise, he was sure they'd all wind up dead, and that was the last thing he wanted.

Country turned back around to Joaquin, looking him in his eyes. "Understood."

Liking that Country had submitted to him, Joaquin nodded approvingly. "Tec, you brought those collars along right?" Aztec nodded and held up the collars with the black square device on it. These were the same collars that the crackheads down in Joaquin's super lab had to wear. Not only did it keep track of its wearer, it acted as an explosive. It would explode once whoever had the remote control to it activated it. "What about the glasses?"

"I got them shits too." Aztec held up two black cases that contained eyeglasses.

"Alright, secure those collars around their necks and release 'em from them cuffs so they can get dressed." Joaquin ordered like the boss nigga he was. Aztec tossed him the remote control to the collars, and he caught it. He then pulled out his SIG Sauer P226 with the silencer, in case Buck Wild and his country ass cousin tried some funny shit.

Joaquin watched as Aztec secured the collars around Buck Wild and Country's necks. He pulled out the handcuff keys and unlocked their metal bracelets, freeing their wrists. They dropped down to the concrete floor and left wet footprints behind, as they rushed over to their piles of clothes. Country was the first of them to get dressed. He ran over to Nadine, giving her and the baby a kiss, and then hugging them emotionally. He promised them that everything was going to be okay, and he was going to get them out of their fucked up situation.

"I love you, shawty." Country kissed Nadine on her forehead.

"I love you too, baby," Nadine replied and wiped the tears falling from her eyes.

Country swept Nadine's individual braids from out of her face, and caressed her cheek with the back of his hand. He was ugly as sin so he couldn't understand how he'd gotten so lucky to hook up with someone so beautiful. Nadine was a short, petite young lady, twenty years of age. She had fair skin and a black mole above her full lips that gave her mad sex appeal. Shorty was shapely with an incredible bust and ass that became more pronounced since she'd been pregnant.

"Alright, enough with all of the romantic shit, y'all get cho asses over here!" Aztec said to Country and Buck Wild, waving them over with his gun.

Country's eyebrows slanted, and his nose scrunched up, hearing the way Aztec was talking to him. He would have given him the burial plot his reckless mouth was asking for had he not been at his mercy. Unfortunately, he was. So he'd have to roll with the punches until he had the upper hand.

"Hang tight, shawty, I'll be back to get you and junior so we can get the fuck from outta here," Country told Nadine, as he continued to caress her cheek with the back of his hand. He then kissed her on the lips and kissed his baby boy on his head, slicking his hair down again.

"Move yo' ass, homeboy, before I put one in it!" Aztec warned him with a scowl. He had every intention of putting a hot one in one of Country's ass cheeks if he didn't come along.

Buck Wild tapped Country and told him in a hushed tone, "Come on, man, let's see what's up with these niggaz."

With that said, Buck Wild and Country walked over to Aztec and Joaquin. Joaquin showed them the remote control/ detonator to the collars they were wearing and explained to them what would happen if they tried anything funny. Afterward, he tucked the remote control in his pocket and handed them the eyeglass cases. As they opened the cases and slipped the glasses on, he told them about the eyeglasses and how they functioned.

"You'll both wear these glasses at all times," Joaquin informed them, watching them look around the basement while wearing the eyeglasses, trying to get a feel for them. "I'll be able to hear and see whatever y'all do. I'll know what's going on the entire time you're gone. Now, if I even think you tryna pulla fast one on me, well, I don't think I needa tell you again what fate lies ahead for you and yo' family." He slipped on a pair of eyeglasses identical to the ones Buck Wild and Country were wearing. In one lens, in a small square box, he could see what Country was seeing and through the other he could see what Buck Wild was seeing. "Yo, hand these niggaz the card with the address to drop God mark-ass off at, Tec." With the word given, Aztec pulled out a white business card from his pocket with the drop-zone's address, and passed it to Country. Country made sure he memorized the address on the card before sticking it inside his pocket. When he looked up, Aztec was tossing him something. He caught it and opened his palm. It was the keys to the whip him and Buck Wild had come there in.

"Alright," Joaquin began, programming the timer on his cell phone. "Y'all fools got an hour and a half, so don't be out there bullshitting. Y'all snatch that dicksucka up and take 'em to the drop-zone. Afterward, you shoot back here, get cho family and ya'll stroll up from outta here."

"That easy, huh?" Buck Wild asked, looking at him like he knew he had something up his sleeve.

"Yep, it's that easy," Joaquin assured him.

"Gemme yo' word, dog, and shake onnit," Country said as he extended his hand.

Joaquin looked at Country's hand and then into his eyes. Reluctantly, he shook his hand while crossing his fingers at his back. There wasn't any way in hell he was going to allow Country and his family to live. He'd already made up his mind that once they'd completed their mission, everybody was getting the business except the baby.

"Alright, y'all get to moving. The sooner you complete the task the sooner you can get cho girl and yo' baby back." Joaquin masked a look of sincerity as he glanced at Country.

Country motioned for Buck Wild to follow him as he treaded up the staircase, Aztec following closely behind them.

***

Madrid pulled up to the park that Stilts told him Aaron would be. Killing his headlights and murdering his engine, he looked back and forth between the picture in his lap and the windshield. His eyes scanned the crowd of young teenagers that were drinking, smoking weed and doing tricks of skateboards. There were exactly four of them in total, all of whom were dressed strangely to him. If they didn't have colorful hair and baggy clothing with wallet chains, then they wore those earrings that stretched their earlobes to incredible lengths. Madrid categorized them as grungy, punk-rocker skater kids from their attire. He'd seen their types many times during his travels in and out of the suburbs of California. Hell, sometimes he'd seen some of the Mexican kids dressed like them.

Madrid scanned the crowd of teenagers, closely trying to make out Aaron's face among them. His eyes jumped back and forth between the kids and the picture of Aaron. He had many tattoos in the photo, but the one that was most noticeable to him was the one on his neck. It was one of a burning skull. It appeared to be 3D, and looked very lifelike. Through Stilts, Madrid found out that Aaron was a rebellious youth with a lengthy rap sheet. He'd never done anything over a month in juvenile hall, on the strength of his father being who he was.

Just another spoiled white kid getting by on his privilege and his daddy's accolades, I've seen this shit a thousand times. Go fucking figure, Madrid thought, as he continued to stare at the picture. He looked out of the driver's window again and narrowed his eyelids, looking closer. He couldn't make out the kid he was looking for from where he was parked, so he'd have to get up close. This wasn't a big deal. He was expecting this. He placed the picture inside the glove box and closed it. Next, he took a gun from underneath the driver's seat and screwed a silencer on its tip. After he stuck the gun inside the holster in his duster, he opened the console and removed a pair of handcuffs. He stuck the handcuffs and the key inside his pocket. He grabbed his hat from off the front passenger seat, and adjusted it on his head. He opened the driver's door, hopped out, and casually strolled across the street to the skate park. The teenagers' conversation and laughter grew louder.

"Aaron Barrett?" Madrid addressed the kid with the dirty blond hair spilling from beneath a beanie with the skull inked on his neck. The boy turned around, taking pulls from the joint wedged between his fingers, smoke crowding him like an early morning fog.

"Do I know you?" Aaron asked and blew out a cloud of smoke his way, disrespectfully.

At that moment, the kid on the skateboard came to a stop beside Aaron, and stomped down on the end of it. The skateboard popped up into the air, and he caught it. He frowned as he looked to his friends, and then to Madrid, wondering what was going on.

"Yo', who's the fuck is this dude?" the skateboard kid asked, motioning a finger at Madrid.

"No, you most definitely don't know me, but I need a favor from your father," Madrid humbly admitted. "And the way I'm going to get that favor is, if I take you as a hostage and demand it."

Aaron and his friends exchanged glances and busted up laughing. A couple of them laughed so hard that they cried and had to wipe away their tears.

"Man, I don't know who the fuck you are, but I suggest you go back to whatever fucking hole you crawled out of—Otherwise, I'm gonna carve a Japanese letter into your forehead," another one of Aaron's friends said as he stepped forward, with a switch blade. He pressed a button on the handle of it, and its sharp metal blade sprung forth. The freckle face kid was wearing a plaid red and black ushanka hat and metal braces on his teeth.

"Kid, I'll take that knife outta your hand, bend you over that railing and fuck you up the ass with it," Madrid threatened with his slanted eyebrows, flaring nostrils and clenched jaws. He could tell by the look in the kid's eyes that he wasn't on that killa shit, but if given a push he may try him. "If I were you, sport, I'd put away my lil' toy, grab my hermanos and take my ass home. Aaron and I have business of our own to attend to." As soon as he said this, another kid wearing a backwards baseball cap and a graphic T-shirt stepped up to the right of him. At the corner of his eye Madrid could see that the youth was holding something. He figured it was either an old water pipe or a branch. Whatever it was, it would surely cause a lot of damage to whomever it was used against.

"I'm done with all of this talking, old man! You're gonna have to show me something!" the kid in the ushanka said, smiling satanically while sliding his tongue across his braces.

Madrid looked from the kid on the side of him to the one standing before him. "Ready when you are, sport."

The kid in the ushanka looked to the one in the graphic T-shirt. That was his signal. The youngsta hoisted up what was a branch, and charged at Madrid at the same his friend that had given the signal did.

"Aaaaaaaah!" the kid in the graphic T-shirt shouted his war cry and prepared to swing the branch.

Madrid kicked the switch blade out of *Ushanka's* hand, and it went up in the air. He ducked as *Graphic T-shirt* swung the branch with all of his might. The branch broke in half on impact and literally broke *Ushanka's* face, knocking him off his feet. Madrid grabbed the switch blade from out of the air and threw it at Aaron. The switch blade spun around with lightning speed, targeting Aaron who'd just cleared a nickel-plated .357 revolver from out of his jeans. He was in the middle of bringing it up when the switch blade landed in his shoulder down to its hilt.

"Aaaaaaaaah!" Aaron threw his head back, wailing in agony and absentmindedly firing his shiny pistol. He dropped his revolver and doubled over, running away, holding his shoulder. As he ran away, he left a trail of burgundy blood behind him, unintentionally.

As soon as Madrid released the switch blade from his hand, he tilted to the side and kicked *Graphic T-shirt* in his chest. The force behind it sent him flying backwards and flipping over the guardrail. He screamed in terror as he plummeted to the cement steps below, snapping his spine. He lay immobilized on the steps, crying out in unbearable pain. By this time, the kid with the skateboard was swinging it at Madrid's head and body. Madrid, moving fluidly, ducked and dodged the skateboard masterfully. He kicked the kid with the skateboard in his chin and launched his head back. He then dipped to the ground, swung his leg around in a 360 degree turn and swept him off his feet. The youngsta fell back to the asphalt, fast and hard, bumping the back of his head. He lay there barely conscious while his skateboard went up into the air and plummeted back down.

Madrid caught the skateboard with one hand, sat it on the ground, and placed his foot on top of it. Looking ahead, he saw Aaron running away and pulling the switch blade from out of his shoulder. Aaron threw the knife aside, continuously looking back over his shoulder as he ran for his life. He found it funny that Madrid was just standing there watching him instead of coming after him. He had it in mind to hop on the bus he saw coming to a stop ahead at the corner.

"Metro, baby, I make it to the bus and I'm home free," Aaron said to no one in particular, with a smile on his face. Meanwhile, Madrid kicked the skateboard in his direction, causing the board to rip up the pavement. The skateboard Madrid sent at him went underneath his foot as it was coming back down. His foot landed on top of the skateboard, carrying him forward and propelling him backward. He went up in the air and landed awkwardly on the side of his neck. He lay where he was hurting and watching the world spin.

Madrid jumped back in his car, busted a U-turn, and raced up the parking lot. He stopped curbside, hopped out while leaving the driver's door open, and popping open the trunk. Walking around the rear of his whip, he pulled out the handcuffs and allowed them to dangle at his side. Using his boot, he pushed Aaron over onto his stomach and held both of his hands behind his back. Looking ahead, he saw the kids he'd put on their asses still lying on the asphalt. He listened to the wailing police car sirens, as he locked the metal bracelets around Aaron's wrists. Madrid hoisted the young man over his shoulder and carried him toward the rear of his car, whistling Dixie. He dumped him inside the trunk, slammed it shut and smacked imaginary dust from his hands. He then hopped inside his car, slammed the door behind him and pulled off.

Chapter 5

Once his vision came into place, he looked from left to right, trying to figure out exactly where he was. From the dirty walls, filthy floor and rusted pipes dripping brown water, it registered in his mind that he was in the bowels of some sort of building. In the shadows of the underground dwelling he spotted several rats sitting on pipes and taking up space in crevasses. The small red orbs that were their eyes watched him closely. There were also several cockroaches crawling around on the pipes, walls and floors. Terrified, his heart thudded behind his chest, its beat resonating in his ears. He tried shouting for help, but the gag in his mouth wouldn't permit it. Hearing ambling around from deep within the darkness, he looked ahead and saw the shadows moving. Three fat ass rats scurried out, squeaking and sniffing around. Madrid came out behind the beady eyed vermin, holding a very lengthy chain that was latched onto something in the shadows. The further he walked inside the room the more of the chain was revealed until the person at the end of it was visible.

"Unh!" a slender white man said aloud as he fell to his knees. The chain was attached to a metal shackle around his neck. Another chain attached to the back of the shackle hung down his back and was attached to the shackles that bound his wrists.

Aaron's eyes widened with surprise when he saw his father. He tried to say something to him, but the gag in his mouth stopped his words from escaping. The only thing that came out were murmurs that grew louder and louder along with the sound of the clinking chains he was dangling from.

"Aaron, Aaron, are you—are you okay, son? Did he hurt you?" the slender white man asked as he struggled to get back upon his feet to engage his son. Old boy was a homicide detective that went by the name Paul Barrett. He was Aaron's father. Madrid had tracked him down using the GPS app in his son's cell phone. Apparently, the boy had the app so he could tell when his pops was anywhere around the area he was in, so he wouldn't catch him doing shit he wasn't supposed to do.

Detective Barrett rocked a shaved head and a five o'clock shadow, with a goatee. He had a mixture of relish, ketchup and mustard on his goatee and button-down shirt. He was strolling toward his Crown Victoria, scoffing down a hotdog, when Madrid sprung out of the shadows and knocked him out cold. When he finally regained consciousness, he had one hell of a migraine and a lump on the back of his head the size of a doorknob. Upon further inspection, he realized he was inside the trunk of his kidnapper's car and wearing the very same chain and shackles he was in now.

"Don't you worry, son, I'm gonna get you outta here, okay? I promise," he said from a kneeling position, kissing his son on his forehead and caressing his cheek affectionately.

Detective Barrett was so occupied with consoling his son that he was oblivious to Madrid approaching him. He held the end of the detective's chain in one hand and a taser in the other. He casually strolled over to him and electrocuted him in the side of his neck. Detective Barrett fell flat on his back, shaking and kicking his legs like a dying cockroach. Seeing his father electrocuted made Aaron scowl with anger. He screamed as loud as he could at Madrid, and struggled to get loose from his chains. No matter how hard he tried, he couldn't manage to release himself from the restraints.

Madrid was standing over Detective Barrett, looking down at him when Aaron stole his attention. He walked over to the young man and tasered him in the neck. The kid's eyes rolled to their whites; he involuntarily shook from where he was hung.

Staring at Aaron, Madrid took a deep breath and stuck the taser inside the pocket of his duster. He connected the end of the chain to a metal loop on the wall and tugged on it twice, making sure it was secure. He walked over to the gray lap top on the floor he'd placed there when he'd first entered the room. He kicked it in Detective Barrett's direction. It slid across the floor and bumped into his arm as he lay on his back, moaning after being shocked.

"Get me all the information I need on Joaquin Torres, twenty-six to twenty-seven years of age—" Madrid said, as he pulled a picture of him and Joaquin from inside of his duster. He walked over to Detective Barrett and dropped it on the floor beside the laptop. "That's him in the picture there, beside me." He pointed the former cartel soldier out with his finger. Afterwards, he unlocked the shackles that bound Detective Barrett's wrists and removed them.

Wincing, Detective Barrett turned over on his side and opened the laptop. After signing in with his password, he logged into the law enforcement database with his information. He typed in Joaquin's first and last name, and a search produced several matches with their picture beside them. Detective Barrett picked up the picture Madrid dropped on the floor beside him and looked at it, committing Joaquin's face to memory. He then looked back at the lap top's screen. Seeing Joaquin's face and his personal information pop up, he clicked on the link provided. Instantly, former addresses and present addresses appeared.

"Here's your guy," Detective Barrett said, as he spun the

lap top around to Madrid.

Madrid, now holding an ink pen and a sheet of paper, picked up the laptop and jotted down every address under Joaquin's name. He then looked up his family which was also in his information. Annabelle Torres came up and then Billie Hoyle came up. Madrid brought up Billie's personal information and jotted down all the addresses under her name as well. Once he was done, he capped his ink pen and put it away. He folded up the sheet of paper and slipped it inside of his pocket. He then closed the laptop and held it at his side.

"Alright, I did like you asked—now let my son and I go—A deal is a deal," Detective Barrett told Madrid, as he sat up from where he was lying.

Madrid reached into the recesses of his duster and pulled out a gun with a silencer on its tip. He extended it toward Aaron's forehead. The boy's eyes bulged fearfully, and he screamed into the gag in his mouth. He swung back and forth on the chain, trying to get free but there wasn't any use.

"What are you doing? No, stop, stoppp!" Detective Barrett screamed as he looked back and forth between Madrid and his son.

Madrid pulled the trigger of his gun, and its silencer whistled as a bullet ripped out of it. Aaron's forehead exploded and created a hole in the back of it. The boy's eyes rolled back to the floor below him, and pieces of his skull, blood and brain fragments dripped below him.

"Nooooooooo! Noooooooo! Noooooooo!" Detective Barrett screamed hysterically over and over again. His face turned red, and veins bulged on his forehead, tears coating his cheeks back to back. He was hurt and angry that Madrid had blown his son's brains out. He whipped his head around to Madrid, mad-dogging him with flaring nostrils. "I'ma kill you, I'ma kill you, you fucking spic! You hear me, you wetback, mothafucka?" He harped up phlegm and spat it at him. The thick disgusting glob splattered on the tip of Madrid's boot. He looked down at it and then back up at Detective Barrett, who was charging at him and screaming hatefully. Madrid lifted up his gun and pointed it at him, lining its barrel up with his forehead. He pulled the trigger, and an empty shell-casing leaped out of the gun. The silencer whistled again, and Detective Barrett's brains splattered out the back of his skull. Madrid lowered his smoking gun and moved out of his path. Detective Barrett crashed to the surface and slid across it, leaving a bloody streak behind. The top of his head bumped up against the wall, and his sliding stopped. A black and a brown roach crawled from off the wall and on to his mangled head. The brown one crawled inside of the hole the bullet made in the back of his dome.

***

While God was gone, Billie went about the task of filling the bullet holes in the walls with Fix All. She softly sang Ashanti's "Baby" as she smoothed the Fix All out over the holes so she could begin painting.

"*I got this jones forming in my bones—from a man/who indeed took over my soul—understand,*" Billie crooned, as she continued to smoothen out the gray gunk over the wall. "*I couldn't breathe if he ever said—he would leave/ get on my knees 'til—*" Billie's brows furrowed, and she stopped smoothening out the gunk. She felt like someone was behind her, so she glanced over her shoulder but there wasn't anyone there. She looked over her other shoulder and didn't find anyone there either. Shrugging, she went back to singing and attending to her task.

"Aaaaaaah!" Billie threw her head back, screaming in agony. She collapsed to the carpeted floor, holding the back of her ankle. Feeling something wet, she looked to her fingers, and they were bloody. She tried to get up on her wounded ankle, and pain shot through it. Looking down at it, she saw that her Achilles tendon had been severed. Hearing hurried footsteps over her shoulder, her head snapped around, and she saw Annabelle coming at her. Her pupils were two balls of fire, her teeth were gritted, and she was clutching a big ass butcher's knife. She snarled as she swung the knife at her mother's throat. Billie threw up her forearm, and the knife sliced into it, spilling blood. "Aaaaaah!" She screamed in agony again. Annabelle straddled her mother and started swinging the knife fast and hard at her face. Billie threw up her arms to block her attack. The knife sliced into the fabric of her sleeve, and her blood dotted up floor and walls.

"Get offa her!" Charity shouted, as she charged at Annabelle. Annabelle whipped around just as she tackled her. They impacted the floor hard and the butcher's knife went flying across the living room. Charity and Annabelle rolled around on the floor, screaming and pulling each other's hair. "What is wrong with you, Anna? Why are you tryna kill your mommy? You're stupid! I wish my mommy was alive!"

"Shut up, shut up, Charity! I swear to god I hate chu and your daddy!" Annabelle shouted at her in a rage. "She's not my mother! She only cares about you, herself and yo' daddy—not mine—and not me—she wants to—she wants to kill 'em!"

"That's not true! Stop lying, you liar!" Charity shouted back, choking her with all her strength and causing her to gag.

"She does—she does—I—I heard her talking to your—your—daddy about—it" Annabelle said, as her eyes built up with tears and a vein bulged at her temple. She began to turn red in the face.

Billie's eyes bulged, and her mouth flung open upon hearing Annabelle's statement. She didn't have any idea she'd heard her and God discussing killing Joaquin. She didn't know what to say to her, or what to do, but she couldn't allow her to harm Charity. With that thought, Billie winced as she began to pull herself up on the wall on her one good leg.

"Liar, liar, liar!" Charity shouted over and over again, spittle raining down on Annabelle's face. Tears spilled down her cheeks as she continued to choke her. She loved and hated her stepsister at the same time. She didn't like the things she was saying about her father because she believed he was a good man. And she didn't like what she was saying about Billie because she looked at her as a mother figure.

"Yes—it—iiiiis!" Annabelle shouted, as she scratched Charity down her face, leaving eight bloody scratches behind. Charity howled in pain and released her neck. Annabelle followed up by punching her in the jaw and sending her flying off of her, to the side. Hurriedly, she sprung to her feet and looked around for the butcher's knife. She smiled devilishly when she spotted it. Snatching it up, she looked at it and saw her reflection. The crimson-stained knife gleamed.

Annabelle looked at Charity, and she was starting to get upon her hand and knees. Touching her bleeding face, she cried as one of her fingers showed faint signs of blood. Annabelle took off, running at her. Right before she reached her, she cocked back her leg and kicked her as hard as she could. Charity winced as she flew two feet and landed hard on her back. Her face was balled up, and she was gritting her teeth, bawling. Seeing her in a vulnerable state, Annabelle decided to take advantage of the situation. She gripped the big butcher's knife like Michael Myers would, and stalked over to her.

"I love you like you my sister Charity, but cho daddy wants my daddy dead," Annabelle said, looking and sounding like someone possessed by a demon than a four-year-old child. Billie, who was slowly hobbling her way over to her, was shocked at how her daughter was behaving. She noticed how much in her temper she looked more like her father when he was angry. The girl most definitely had his short temper, and apparently his killer edge as well. "He's tryna hurt me by killing him. So I'ma kill you and hurt him!"

Annabelle shrilled as she charged toward Charity to finish her off. She'd gotten halfway across the living room floor before Billie landed a backhand slap in her face. The butcher's knife flew out of Annabelle's hand, as she hurled across the living room. She crashed to the carpeted floor and tumbled toward the door, landing up against it. Annabelle sat slumped up against the front door with a red welt on her cheek from the assault. Slowly, she lifted her head and looked up at her mother who was lying on the floor. She'd fallen there after slapping her. Annabelle was dizzy, and her vision had gone blurry. She moaned because of her aching head. She felt the back of her head and looked at her hand, but there was no bloodstain.

"Uhhhh!" Billie sat up and looked at Charity who was sitting up as well. "Are you—are you okay, lil' mama?"

"Yeah," Charity responded as she nodded, rubbing her aching side. "I'm okay."

Charity got upon her feet and ran over to Billie. She hugged her affectionately and kissed her on the cheek. Billie smiled and rubbed her back with her free hand. Seeing the blood running from her stepmother's Achilles tendon made Charity's eyes widen. She couldn't believe how badly she was bleeding.

"Oh, my god, did—did Anna do that to you?" Charity asked, looking down at her foot. She'd never seen so much blood in her entire life. Surprisingly, Billie's wounded ankle looked just like the ones she'd seen in motion pictures. She wanted to touch it to see how it felt, but she feared she'd hurt her stepmother. She definitely didn't want to do that.

A look of worry spread across Billie's face, seeing Annabelle get upon her feet. She looked from her to the butcher's knife that flew across the living room when she assaulted her. Looking to Charity, she told her to retrieve the butcher's knife and bring it over to her. When Charity saw Annabelle up on her feet, she knew things could get ugly again so she hurriedly recovered the butcher's knife. She handed it to Billie and got down on her knees beside her, holding onto her arm.

"Pretty girl, have you calmed down now?" Billie asked her daughter. Annabelle stood there as still as a statue, head tilted downward, giving her evil eyes, clenching her small fists at her sides. She looked like an angry Chihuahua that couldn't wait to get out of its owner's yard and chew someone's ass up. "Pretty girl, do you hear me talking to you? Huh?" Again, Annabelle didn't reply. Instead, she stood her ground, gritting her teeth and balling her fists tighter.

"I hate chu, I hate chu, I hate chu!" Annabelle shouted over and over again, with spit flying from her lips. The veins on her forehead and neck throbbed and looked like they were ready to erupt.

"Sweetheart, you must have been dreaming or

something. I assure you that's not what chu heard." Billie lied with a straight face, trying her best to convince her daughter. This was the only trick she had up her sleeve, so she hoped it worked. "Why would I wanna kill your father when I know how much you love him? I know me or Kyree would not do something like that, knowing full well it would hurt chu. And I don't wanna hurt my pretty girl, I love you too much, baby. Come here." She extended her arm to her daughter to receive her, but she wasn't budging.

"You think I'm stupid, huh?" Annabelle asked, folding her arms across her chest.

"No, baby, you're definitely smart. Mommy didn't raise any dummies."

"If that's the case then why are you trying to play me like a dummy, huh? I heard y'all. I heard y'all both." Annabelle knew what she heard, and she wasn't backing down from her mother. There wasn't any way in hell she was going to convince her that she'd heard otherwise. She was a lot of things, but stupid wasn't one of them. Hell, she'd learned to read and add at the tender age of two. She was smarter and more intelligent than a lot of children her age. Her parents made sure of that during her upbringing.

"Baby, I promise, that's not what chu heard. You hadda been half asleep or something. Your stepfather and I never had that discussion." Billie was lying so goddamn good that she had Annabelle questioning whether she'd heard right or not. Right then, the front door came unlocked and God walked inside, locking the door behind him. He looked from Billie's wounded ankle to Annabelle as he placed his car keys in his pocket, wondering what the hell had happened while he was gone.

"What's going in here?" God asked curiously.

Billie gave God the rundown on what had occurred and

why it had happened. He looked at Billie like he couldn't believe Annabelle overheard their conversation, but he knew to play it off. Little mama was still young, so it was possible for them to trick her into believing she hadn't heard right.

God kneeled down to Annabelle, holding her hands and looking into her eyes. "Lil' mama, I know that you know that your father and I have our issues with each other. But I swear on my life that I'm not gonna kill 'em. You have my word that I will not kill your father." He looked her dead in her eyes. She held his gaze, and she suddenly broke down, crying. He hugged her and lifted her up. "There, there now. It's okay. I know you're tired and confused. Everything is gonna be okay." He looked to Charity and extended his hand toward her. She got to her feet and ran over to him, grasping his hand. "Babe, I'ma lay them down and tuck 'em in so they can get some sleep. Then, I'ma see about having Kershawn come by here to watch them so I can take you to the hospital."

"Okay," Billie said as she nodded. She pulled herself up by the back of the couch and hobbled over to the front of it, plopping down on its cushiony seats. God kissed her as he passed her, carrying the girls off to bed. Once he'd tucked them in and kissed them goodnight, he returned to the living room.

God sat on the arm of the couch and pulled out his cellular, searching for Kershawn's contact. He was about to hit him up when he heard a knock at the door. He exchanged looks of astonishment with Billie, and then looked to the door. Stashing his cell phone in his pocket, he withdrew his gun and approached the door with stealth. His body was tense as he peered through the peephole, but he relaxed once he saw Buck Wild and Country on the other side of the door.

"Who is it?" Billie asked in a hushed tone.

"Buck Wild and Country with their late asses," God answered, as he stuck his gun back on his waistline. He unlocked the door and dapped up his homies as they fell into his house. He locked the door behind them. "Where the fuck have y'all been, man?" he asked, as he disappeared inside the hallway, listening to them as he went to retrieve something.

"Man, one of the spots got robbed, bruh," Country told him.

"Get the fuck outta here," God said from inside the bathroom.

"Real spit, dog—We think it may be someone on the inside," Buck Wild chimed in.

"Yeah? Who's that?"

"That young nigga we just put on—" Buck Wild said.

"What young nigga, bruh? Fuck you beating around the bush for? Spit that shit out, nigga," God said as he emerged into the living room with a yellow first-aid kit. He carried it over to the couch where Billie was perched, and sat down beside her. He sat it down on the coffee table and popped its locks, lifting its lid. He sat the items he was going to use to clean Billie's wound on the table top and two beige rolls of ace bandages. "My nigga, who are we talking about here?"

"Yo', what the fuck happened to yo' shawty?" Country asked with a furrowed brow, looking concerned.

"It's a long ass story, dog—One we really don't have time to tell," God said. As he cleaned drying blood around Billie's wound, she flinched and hissed like a serpent. "My bad, ma—Buck, what's the holdup witchu, bruh?"

"Flex," Buck Wild told him regretfully.

Frowning, God stopped cleaning Billie's wound and looked at Buck Wild. "Flex the tall pretty boy nigga with a tapered fade?" He motioned his palm over his head when he mentioned the kid's hair.

"Yeah, that's him." Buck Wild nodded.

"Buck, you handpicked the young nigga ya self. Said you give yo' right hand that he was a standup dude." God went back to cleaning Billie's wound. "You know the rules when you bring someone new into the organization and they prove to be disloyal."

"You gotta take 'em out yo' self," Buck Wild and Country said in unison.

"That's right. So, I take it you're here to tell me that y'all done smoked his lil' thieving-ass, right?" God said, as he applied ointment around Billie's wound with a Q-tip. She winced on and off, as he administered the clear jelly.

"Nah, he won't tell us where the work he stole is at?" Buck Wild admitted.

"Yeah, mothafucka said he won't talk to anyone but you," Country added to the discussion. "If you ask me, I think he's tryna bargain his way outta his predicament. You know, on some *I'll tell you where the weight at if you promise to let me go.*"

"That's outta the fucking question. I let that young, dumb mothafucka skate then other niggaz gon' start thinking shit sweet and try to run off with my product too." God hissed. "Fuck naw! I'ma tell his ass whatever he wants to hear so I can get my shit back and then Buck is gonna put a cap in ol' monkey ass." He said all of these words without even turning around. He was still busy with Billie's wound, packing it with dressing so he could eventually wrap it up and take her to the hospital. "Where y'all got this nigga at anyway?"

Buck Wild and Country exchanged glances like they were reluctant to break the news to him. When he didn't hear a reply, God stopped dressing Billie's wound and turned around to them. "Well, where the fuck is he?"

"He's outside in the trunk of the car." Buck Wild informed him.

God looked at Buck Wild and Country like they were Dumb and Dumber. "I know fucking well you two fucking geniuses didn't bring the victim of a goddamn kidnapping over to my crib." He watched as Buck Wild and Country exchanged glances and looked back at him, nodding *yes*. "I should kick y'all asses, especially yours Buck 'cause yo' ass know better, man. I expect shit like this from Country, but chu 'pose to be the brains of y'all lil' outfit. Fuck!" He leaned his head back and slid his hands down his face. Frustrated, he blew his breath and looked to Billie. "Baby, I'ma roll with these fools to handle this business right quick. I want chu to holla at cho uncle to see if he can have Humphrey watch the girls while he take you to the hospital. Okay?" Billie nodded yes. "Thanks, babe," he told her and wrapped her leg up with the ace bandages, making sure they held firmly. He then kissed her and hopped up from the couch, heading to the front door. "Y'all niggaz, come on, man," he told Buck Wild and Country, as he walked past them. "What the fuck is that around yo' neck, Country?"

A guilt look came over Country's face as he exchanged glances with Buck Wild. He pulled the collar of his shirt up over the black GPS/explosive device that Aztec secured around his neck. "It's a choker, nigga. Me and Buck got one. It's the latest shit in fashion—everyone's rocking them now. You betta get onnit."

"No, thank you—Not my style," God told him. He frowned when he saw the glasses they were wearing. He hadn't noticed them before because he was so engrossed in tending to Billie's wound. "I guess them silly ass glasses is a part of the latest fashion also, huh?" he asked as they treaded toward their car.

"Yep," Buck Wild grinned and adjusted the eyeglasses that Joaquin had given them. He knew it was likely he was seeing what they were seeing right now.

"Y'all fucking taste sucks." God shook his head, thinking about his boys' accessories. "Yo, y'all ain't said a word about what happened to our friend." He referred to Joaquin who he'd sent them to murder.

"Ya boy pushing up daisy's, shawty," Country chimed in.

"Yeah, we did 'em quick, too—Caught his bitch-ass while he was in the shower and sprayed 'em like the cockroach he is," Buck Wild said. He and Country looked at each other through their peripherals. The bullshit they were feeding God sounded so believable they'd almost convinced themselves they were telling the truth.

"My niggaz," God smiled as he hung his arms around their shoulders. "I knew I could count on you mothafuckaz. That lil' deed y'all did for me counts as good credit towards this fuck-up y'all brought me tonight." He said this as they crossed the street and headed to their whip.

Country, Buck Wild and God piled inside of the whip. Country drove while God chilled on the passenger side. He stared out of the window as he smoked the half of blunt he'd found in the ashtray. The wind was blowing against him so hard that he had to narrow his eyelids, embers flying from the tip of his bleezy. Country looked up into the rearview mirror and met Buck Wild's eyes. They gave each other a nod, letting each other know it was time to make their move.

"It's quiet as a bitch in here, bruh—I hate silence," Country said to no one in particular, as he turned on the stereo. He found a song he was feeling, and cranked its volume up high. He glanced up in the rearview mirror at

Buck Wild whom he saw was busy doing something he couldn't see.

Buck Wild held a folded black bandana in the palm of his hand, soaking it with chloroform. He twisted the cap back on the bottle and sat it on the floor between his legs. Scooting to the edge of his seat, he snatched God back against the headrest by his forehead and held the bandana over his nose and mouth. God struggled to break his hold to no avail. After a while, his eyelids fluttered and he started moving slower and slower until he eventually went still. Just to be sure he was really out cold, Buck Wild held the bandana to him a minute longer and then released him.

"He's out, man—Pull over so we can tie 'em up and dump 'em in the trunk," Buck Wild told his cousin. "The man said as soon as we get 'em to the drop-zone and get back to 'em, then the sooner we can get these uncomfortable ass collars from around our necks." He tugged at the strap of the collar. It felt like a fucking noose around his neck, and he hated that shit.

"Good, 'cause this bitch got me itching like crazy—scratching like a goddamn flea-bitten dog," Country complained, as he tried to scratch underneath the strap of the collar.

Chapter 6

When Billie told Kershawn Annabelle was the culprit that had slashed her Achilles tendon, he was shocked. He couldn't believe his darling niece would do such a thing. He'd always looked at her as sweet little angel, but apparently, he was wrong. Annabelle Torres was indeed a devil in disguise. Although Kershawn had a million and one questions he wanted to ask Billie, he figured it was best to ask them on the way to the hospital. Billie's blood was beginning to seep through the bandages so he'd have to get her some medical attention as soon as possible. Seeing Billie had trouble walking on her injured foot, Kershawn scooped her up in his arms and carried her out of the house. She waved goodbye to Humphrey and made him promise to protect the girls with his life, to which he swore he would.

Once Billie and Kershawn were gone, Humphrey decided to make himself at home like Billie had suggested to him. After hanging up his apple jack and blazer, he headed inside the kitchen where he fixed himself a hot cup of apple cinnamon tea. Journeying out of the kitchen, he dipped the tea-bag repeatedly in the steaming cup. Picking up the remote control, he sat down on the couch and turned on the television. He flipped through the channels until he came across the news. He sipped his cup of tea while watching the news, occasionally seeing his reflection on the screen.

Lipton Humphrey was a forty-eight-year-old white man of British descent. He had a thick nest of silver hair which he wore slicked back. His receding hairline made his forehead appear larger than it actually was. He had a thick mustache that curled over his top lip, wrinkles around his eyes and mouth, and loose skin around his throat area. Humphrey was enjoying his tea when he heard the doorbell chime. He glanced at his watch and wondered who'd be dropping by ten o'clock at night. Figuring it was trouble at that hour, he sat the cup down on the coffee table, and peeled himself up from the couch.

"Who is it?" Humphrey asked, as he approached the front door, pulling his gun from his brown leather holster.

"Police!" a voice said from the other side of the door.

Humphrey glanced through the peephole and, sure enough, there was a police officer standing outside of the door. He stuck his gun back inside of its holster and went about the task of unchaining and unlocking the door. He pulled the door open just enough so he could peer out, taking in the full scope of the police officer. He was an older gentleman of possibly Mexican heritage, and he looked quite menacing, like he fit more breaking the law than enforcing it.

"Good evening, officer, wut seems ta be tha problem, suh?" Humphrey asked in his British accent. The officer was giving him his reason for being there, but he wasn't hearing him. His attention was focused on the fading tattoo on his forearm. It was of the grim reaper holding an AK-47 and a machete in the form of an X against his chest. The machete was dripping with blood. Above the grim reaper in red ink was 'Blood Brothers' and below the grim reaper was 'Cartel' which was bleeding.

Humphrey was very familiar with The Blood Brothers Cartel. Not only had they'd received nationwide news coverage for the heinous acts they'd committed in Mexico, but Joaquin, the man his boss's niece and husband were warring with, was a member of their organization sometime in the past. Humphrey believed then that Joaquin had probably sent the man there to kidnap the girls, and he couldn't allow that to happen because he'd sworn to protect them with his life.

The police officer was none other than Madrid. His forehead wrinkled, as he wondered what Humphrey was looking at. He looked at the tattoo on his forearm and then at the old Brit. Through their eyes they communicated that they knew he wasn't an actual police officer. Humphrey went to draw his gun from its holster at the same time that Madrid kicked the door with all his might. The door slammed into Humphrey's face and broke his nose, bloodying the lower half of his face. The old Brit stumbled backward and fell to the floor. There was purplish black bruising around Humphrey's nose from his nose being fractured, and his face was pink with pain.

"Oh, my god, Humphrey!" Charity cried and smacked her hand over her mouth. Her eyes watered, seeing what had happened to the old man. Annabelle was standing beside her, and she was shocked to see what had happened.

"Go, girls! Get outta here! Get outta here now!" Humphrey yelled at the girls, as he slowly got upon his feet.

Charity and Annabelle darted toward the front door, but Madrid slammed it shut and locked it. The girls turned around and ran back inside of their parents' bedroom.

"Where's Joaquin?" Madrid asked, as he advanced in Humphrey's direction.

When he asked this, Humphrey looked at Madrid in confusion. He initially thought he was there on Joaquin's behalf, but now he knew that wasn't the case.

"I don't know, and I don't care, bru," Humphrey said, as he finally got upon his feet into a martial arts fighting stance. "Ya fucked up tha moment ya broke inta my loved ones house, eh? Let's get to it." He threw up his fists and stared down Madrid as blood dripped from his chin, splashing on the carpeted floor.

Madrid smiled devilishly. It had been a while since he'd

had a good old-fashioned brawl. He'd been retired from the street life for quite some time, so he was anxious to see how he'd fare against the man standing before him.

"Yes, let's," Madrid said, as he got into a fighting stance and held up his fists.

Humphrey came at Madrid, swinging his left, his right and then whipping around with a kick. Madrid caught his foot, and the old man swung his other foot around. The heel of his shoe slammed into Madrid's jaw and sent blood flying out of his mouth. Both of the men fell to the floor, but Humphrey was the first to get up. He was trying to finish his opponent off as quickly as possible. Humphrey lifted his leg high into the air and swung the heel of his shoe down with all of his might. Madrid blocked it with his forearm and kicked him in his balls. The old Brit's eyes bulged, and he hollered out in excruciation. He staggered backward, doubled over, holding himself. Madrid got upon his feet. He charged forward and kicked Humphrey in his chin. Humphrey flipped over the couch and landed on the glass coffee table, shattering it into pieces.

"Uhhhh!" Humphrey groaned in pain, as he attempted to get upon his feet, slicing his hands on the broken glass. He was bleeding awfully by the mouth, slimy ropes of blood hanging from his chin. When he looked back up at Madrid, he was seeing double, but he was still going to try to defend himself. Humphrey took two swings at Madrid which he ducked with ease. Madrid followed up with two haymakers which whipped his head from left to right, splattering his blood on the television screen. Humphrey staggered backward and fell in a flash. Madrid snatched him up and started slamming him face first into the walls, the kitchen table, the refrigerator and the counter top. He even opened up the refrigerator door, placed Humphrey's head into the doorway of it, and slamming the door into it several times.

Madrid released the collar of Humphrey's shirt, and he fell to the kitchen floor. Humphrey's face was bruised and dripping blood on the floor. He had a look on his face like he was drunk, but he was actually dizzy. He grabbed hold of Madrid's pants leg and tried to pull himself up. Madrid yanked his leg back, and kicked him in the side of his head, causing an eerie siren to blare in his ear. Humphrey fell to the floor, blinking his bloodshot eyes. Again, he tried to get up on his feet, but it felt like the entire room was spinning. Every time he tried to get up, he'd wind up falling back down and trying all over again.

Madrid grabbed him by the back of his collar and by his crotch, squeezing his balls. Humphrey howled in pain, feeling his testicles being crushed, but he was too weak to fight his attacker off. With all his strength, Madrid swung the old Brit down against his bending knee. His spine made a loud snap that sounded like crab legs being cracked open. Madrid let go of Humphrey, and he fell to the floor on his stomach. There were veins bulging over his forehead, and his face was completely red, like it had been painted. The agony he felt was something he'd never experienced before, and he knew that most likely this was his last hurrah!

Madrid casually walked over to Humphrey who was reaching for the gun inside of his blazer. The old Brit pulled out his gun and tried to point it at his attacker. Madrid grabbed him by his wrist and placed his finger on top of his finger which was on the trigger. Humphrey grimaced as he tried to stop him from turning the gun against him, but his efforts were to no avail. The beating he'd taken had left him seriously weakened and at his attacker's mercy. Madrid smiled satanically, as he forced Humphrey's own gun inside of his mouth. The fear in the old Brit's eyes gave him a sick sense of joy. He watched the fire of the fight die in his eyes, and then he pulled the trigger.

Blocka!

Specs of blood clung to Madrid's face as he blew out the back of Humphrey's head. He let his lifeless body drop to the floor and then he stepped over him, heading to the back of the house, to find the girls.

"It's okay, lil' ladies, Madrid is not gonna hurt chu. I just wanna talk, that's all. I promise." Madrid lied, as he walked toward the hallway. He stopped short when a scowling Annabelle ran out into the hallway with a .45 automatic. It was the same gun God had given her mother to stash for him. The gun was black and had a silencer on its barrel. It seemed to be heavier than she was because she was trying trouble holding it. She clutched the .45 with both hands. It took her two tries to finally hoist it up and point it up at Madrid. He smiled, looking at her struggle to hold the gun. He really didn't take her seriously.

"Ah, you're so hermosa, you must be Joaquin's mija," Madrid told her, taking slow and calculated steps towards her. "You don't look exactly like 'em, but right here—right now—balling your face up like that—you definitely mirror him."

"Entraste en la casa equivocada, idiota! (*You broke into the wrong house, asshole!*)" Annabelle spat venomously and pulled the trigger. Fire spat out of the .45 and the blowback sent her flying backward down the hallway. The shot went wild and snatched off the lower half of Madrid's earlobe. He winced from the burning sensation he felt. He couldn't believe that the little girl had the guts to take a shot at him. He'd clearly underestimated her, but he should have known better. After all, she did have the blood of a killa flowing through her veins.

Madrid touched what was left of his ear and looked at his fingertips. They were bloody. He looked down the hallway at Annabelle, and she'd gotten back upon her feet, hoisting the gun up again. He was about to shoot her, but he realized he'd need her alive to lure in Joaquin. With that in mind, Madrid charged at Annabelle. He'd closed the distance between them halfway when she pulled the trigger again.

Choot!

The .45 spat fire and sent Annabelle flying backward again. She crashed to the carpeted floor, and the bullet slammed Madrid high in his chest. Madrid stumbled backward and tried to grab hold of something to stop his fall. Unable to latch on to anything, he fell to the floor on his back, grimacing and feeling underneath the bullet-proof vest he was wearing.

"Maldita sea, eso duele muchísimo! ¡Hijo de puta!(*Goddamn that hurts like hell! Son of a bitch!*)" Madrid bawled on the floor in agony.

Charity stuck her head out into the hallway from her parents' bedroom door. Her eyes were pink, and her cheeks were slicked wet with tears.

"Is the—is the bad man dead yet?" Charity asked and sniffled, wiping her teary eyes with her curled finger.

"Not yet! Now get cho scary butt back in the room and close and lock the door, like I told you," Annabelle told her angrily. She was almost as fearless as her father, and being that she was older than Charity by four months, she felt that it was her duty to protect her.

Hearing Madrid bawling in pain down the hallway, Charity looked at him. She became scared, seeing that he was still alive and moving. She ran back inside of the bedroom and locked the door behind her. Once Charity was gone, Annabelle—holding the warm .45 automatic handgun with both hands—cautiously approached Madrid with plans to dome him.

I've gotta shoot 'em in the head. That's what they do in the movies to make sure someone is dead—they shoot 'em in the head. I can do it. If Billie and Papi can do it then I can do it. I am their daughter, and if they can kill someone then I can too, Annabelle thought, as she crept toward Madrid while he continued to bawl on the floor. It was from her eavesdropping that she'd found out loads of things that she shouldn't have the knowledge of. She'd discovered that her father was one of the top enforcers of a notorious cartel in Mexico. That her mother and Uncle Kershawn were highly trained assassins, and that her stepfather Kyree was a drug lord who was known as *God* in the streets.

Annabelle towered over Madrid and took a deep breath, pointing her .45 at his temple. She was about to pull the trigger, when he abruptly smacked the gun out of her hand. Once he smacked the gun out of her hand, his other hand came into play, going across her face viciously. Annabelle hit the carpeted floor, wincing and holding her stinging red cheek. She had tears in her eyes but she refused to cry. She wanted to be like she'd heard her father was: heartless and without feelings.

Still rubbing the sore area underneath his bullet-proof vest, Madrid got upon his booted feet, looking down at Annabelle. He smirked at the corner of his lips, thinking of how deadly she was at such a young age.

"You're such a brave soul, lil' one, your padre would be so proud," Madrid said, as he grabbed Annabelle up by the collar of her shirt, dangling her from his balled fists. She swung and kicked at him to no avail. Giving up, she harped up a glob of spit and spat in his face. Madrid wiped the spit from his face with his fist. He then pulled a syringe out of his pocket, pulled off its cap and spat it aside. Holding it up, he squirted some of the contents of its tip and slid its needle inside a thick vein in Annabelle's neck. She winced, feeling the sharp metal pierce her skin. Madrid pushed down on the plunger and flooded the child's bloodstream with the sedative.

"What did you shoot me with, huh? What did you put—in—my—my bo—dy?" Annabelle's eyes fluttered until they eventually shut, and her voice trailed off. She went limp in Madrid's fist, and she hung like a Christmas ornament from his arm.

Once Annabelle was asleep, Madrid laid her down gently on the couch and removed another syringe from his pocket. Again, he pulled off the cap with his teeth and spat it aside. Holding the syringe behind his back, he slowly made his way down the hallway toward God and Billie's bedroom.

"It's okay, lil' one, I'm not here to hurt chu. You shouldn't be afraid to come out." Madrid spoke with a calm soothing tone. He stopped at God and Billie's bedroom door and pressed his ear against it, listening closely. His eyes moved from side to side, as he tried to hear what was going on inside, but he didn't hear anything. He twisted the doorknob and found that it was locked. "Open the door, mama; I just wanna talk, okay? Open the door for your Uncle Madrid." He waited for a minute to see if Charity was going to answer the door, but she never did. "Alright, I tried to be nice, but I see now that's not getting me anywhere, so allow me to introduce you to the Blood Brothers Cartel numbre uno enforcer—El Boogeyman!"

Boom!

Madrid kicked in the bedroom door, and part of the frame flew inward. Madrid stormed inside of the bedroom wide eyed, pupils dancing with madness. His face was sweaty, and he was gritting his teeth. He looked like he'd gone insane, as he scanned the bedroom for Charity. He rushed over to the bed and flipped over the mattress, letting it fall up against the wall. He tossed the box spring aside and was surprised he didn't find Charity there. Standing upright, chest heaving up and down, Madrid listened closely for Charity. A satanic smile curled the ends of his lips as his neck craned to the closet door, where he could hear her whimpering. He stalked over to the closet door and snatched it open. The cries went silent. Using one hand, he started yanking clothes from off the pole they were hanging on until Charity became visible. She was cowering at the corner of the closet. She made eye contact with Madrid's crazy-looking ass, and she started screaming louder and louder. She continued to scream, scratching and kicking at him as he reached out to her. He winced as her scratch broke his skin and caused him to bleed. He clenched his jaws to combat the burning sensation in his arm, and continued to reach for her.

"Come here! Come here, bring yo' lil' ass here!" Madrid said grumpily, as he finally grabbed a fistful of Charity's hair. He pulled her out of the closet while she kept kicking and screaming. He pinned her up against the wall and slid the needle of the syringe into her neck, pressing the plunger all the way down. The contents of the syringe emptied out into Charity's bloodstream, and took her out of the fight.

Madrid threw Charity over his shoulder and treaded out of the bedroom, whistling Dixie. He laid her down on the couch beside Annabelle. Searching underneath the kitchen cabinet, he found a tool box which he promptly opened. He smiled happily when he saw a length of rope, which he wrapped around his fists. He coiled and uncoiled the rope to test its strength. It was good and sturdy, perfect for keeping the girls' wrists bound. Madrid tied up the girls' wrists and searched the house for something to gag their mouths with. Coming across two bandanas inside God and Billie's bedroom, he used them to gag Charity and Annabelle's mouths. Afterward, he tucked a girl under each arm and carried them out of the house. He dumped the girls into the trunk of his vehicle and slammed it shut. Hopping in behind the wheel, he cranked up his whip and drove off, listening to Dean Martin's "Ain't That a Kick in the Head".

***

Joaquin's cellular rang, and he saw a number he wasn't familiar with. He started to dismiss the call, but something at the front of his mind told him he should answer it.

"Hola," Joaquin spoke into the receiver.

"Hola, hijo, mucho tiempo sin hablar. Cómo estás? (*Hello, son, long time no talk. How are you?*)" The caller greeted jovially with an edge of evilness to his voice.

Joaquin went silent for a moment, hearing the familiar voice. There wasn't any mistaking who he was on the jack with. The voice belonged to someone he once looked at as a friend, but something told him they were foes now.

"Qué pasa? El gato te comió la lengua?(*What's the matter? Cat got your tongue?*)" the caller asked.

"How did you get my number, Madrid?" Joaquin asked, as he began pacing the floor. He was listening to Madrid, but keeping an eye on Nadine and her baby as well.

"Your daughter gave it to me."

Joaquin stopped his pacing. His heart raced, and his stomach twisted in knots. He'd heard what he said, but he seriously hoped he was mistaken. "Fuck you just say?"

"Daddy, you've gotta save me! This man that says he's your uncle kidnapped—" Annabelle was cut short.

Joaquin's face wrinkled with rage. He clenched his teeth and balled his fist. At this time, Aztec returned to the basement with a furrowed brow. He saw the look on Joaquin's face, and he wondered what was going on. He was about to say something to him, but Joaquin held up his finger for him to give him a minute.

"You son of a bitch, I swear to god, if you hurt my baby I'll—"

"I don't have any intentions of hurting your daughter, or her lil' friend, if you show up to my location—alone," Madrid assured him.

"What the fuck is this about?" Joaquin asked, scratching his temple.

Madrid ignored his question and gave him the address to his location. He then disconnected the call.

"Hello? Hello? Hello? Fuck!" Joaquin started pacing the floor impatiently, running his hand down his face. He was worried, really worried. He'd worked side by side with Madrid, and they'd done some shockingly wicked shit together that he was sure bought their way into hell. Joaquin had tried his best to forget some of the heinous acts he'd done, but his mind wouldn't allow him to. This was why he'd turned to alcohol and drugs to get by. Although he'd done an awful lot of evil deeds in his lifetime, there was one in particular that would always stick with him.

On one occasion, Joaquin and Madrid had kidnapped the child of a rival cartel boss and tied him up inside the basement of an old abandoned house. Madrid smeared the boy's penis and testicles with peanut butter and set up a video camera to film what would take place overnight. When they came back the next morning, they found the youth's body and legs covered in bloody bite marks. That wasn't the worse of it; rats had eaten the child's penis and testicles completely off. What really surprised them was the boy was still alive. The kid looked at them with pleading eyes and begged for them to kill him. Madrid didn't feel any remorse for what he'd done. In fact, he was going to leave the boy there to suffer until he died until Joaquin persuaded him to put him out of his misery. Reluctantly, Madrid put a bullet in the child's head and left him behind for the rats to finish devouring. The footage got into the hands of the rival cartel boss's hands, and his guilt led him to committed suicide by hanging.

"Hermano, what's up?" Aztec asked with concern written across his face.

"My mija, she's been kidnapped," Joaquin told him, regretfully.

Aztec looked over his shoulder and narrowed his eyelids at Nadine. She was grinning while still breastfeeding her baby.

"What the fuck about this do you find funny?" Aztec asked heatedly, scrunching his face and flaring his nostrils. Joaquin turned around to Nadine, and he wasn't feeling the grin on her face either. He was as hot as fish grease and wanted to smack fire out of her ass, but he had to check himself. He'd fuck around and kill her, but he needed her as leverage.

"No. I don't find anything funny about your situation, but I do find it ironic," Nadine told them. "Someone has kidnapped this man's daughter, and he's worried about her safety. Just how he had my baby and I kidnapped and my man is now worried about our safety—out there doing all he can to guarantee we both make it outta here alive." She raised her eyebrows and twisted her lips, tilting her head to the side. She was looking at them. *You don't like how that shit feels, huh*? she thought.

"That's it. I'm 'bouta pistol-whip that grin right off that bitch." Aztec frowned and turned his gun over in his hand so he'd be holding it by its barrel. He nudged Joaquin aside saying, "Pardon me, bro." He started in Nadine's direction, but Joaquin grabbed him by his arm.

"Nah, she's right, bro. What goes around comes around."

Aztec nodded understandingly and said, "Youz a lucky bitch. You should be kissing my bro's ass right now." He wagged the handle of his gun at her.

"Listen," Joaquin began in a hushed tone that only Aztec could hear. "This mothafucka wants me to come holla at him on some solo shit in order for me to get my baby girl back. So, I'ma need you to hold shit down here for me until I get back."

"I got chu faded, bro," Aztec said, dapping up Joaquin and giving him a brotherly hug. "Hit me up if you need me, dog."

"Fa sho'," Joaquin replied as he headed up the staircase, adjusting his eyeglasses.

***

Unconscious, God sat with his head bowed strapped to an iron chair. Droplets of water fell from the worn holes in the warehouse's ceiling and splashed on the wet ground, adding to the dirty puddles of water already present. There were old, rusted fifty gallon barrels of burning wood shards with embers flying around them, looking like fireflies. The fires of the barrels kept the building well-lit and somewhat warm, which La'Quan and Marquette—the men who were commissioned to torture and murder God—were thankful for.

La'Quan removed the cap of a tube and moved it back and forth underneath God's nose. His head snapped up, and he looked around, trying to figure out where he was. When he saw he was in an abandoned warehouse with La'Quan and Marquette, his face scrunched up angrily.

"'Bout time you woke up, you just missed yo' boys too," Marquette told him. "They just left."

"The last thing this brotha needs to be worrying about is old acquaintances," La'Quan said, keeping his soulless eyes on God, as he unsheathed his katana from his back. He pressed his thumb against the tip of the slightly curved sword, and a bubble of blood formed. After he sucked the blood off his thumb, he looked at God and smiled evilly. "But if he is worrying about them, once I start chopping off body parts he'll forget *alllllll* about them—I promise."

A gleam swept up the entire length of La'Quan's katana as he looked at it, admiringly. He walked toward God, swinging the razor-sharp blade, listening as it sliced back and forth through the air. He stopped in front of God. Holding his sword in both hands, he lifted it up and brought it right above his shoulder blade. He was practicing how he was going to chop off his left arm. He did this three times, but God didn't even flinch. He kept his angry eyes on him, looking like he was the least worried about what he was going to do to him.

Marquette stood aside with his arms folded across his chest, smiling in satisfaction, observing the entire ordeal.

"Gangsta 'til the end, huh? Well, we're gonna see about that," La'Quan told God, as he lifted his katana high above his head. His face twisted into a mask of evilness, and he smiled, licking his lips. "Brace yourself 'cause this is gonna hurt. Oh, yeah, this is gonna hurt bad. I mean, real, real bad!" He was about to swing his katana into God's shoulder blade when the sound of the warehouse's shutter bursting open startled him. Two black-on-black Mercedes Benz vans with bright headlights sped inside. Still holding the sword above his head, La'Quan looked around, shocked, wondering what the fuck was going on. Seeing an open window of opportunity, God, with the chair still strapped to him, tackled La'Quan to the ground. They hit the surface hard and the katana slid across the ground, spinning around in circles. Right then, the Mercedes Benz vans were halting to a stop. Niggaz wearing ski-masks and black fatigues hopped out armed with machine guns with infrared lasers on them. Their booted feet hit the ground, and they started moving around strategically. Their movements were fast and seemed choreographed, like they'd been training for situations like this.

Marquette's head whipped from left to right, watching the masked men forming a circle around them. Not knowing what the fuck was going on, he pulled a MAC-10 from around his back and cocked a bullet into it. He'd just pointed the black compact machine gun at God, when what seemed like one thousand red dots appeared on his body. He looked down at the red dots covering him from head to toe. He dropped the MAC-10 and slowly raised his hands up in the air. His eyes narrowed into slits, and he frowned, blinded by the bright headlights of the vans. He was at the masked men's mercy and wondering what was to come next.

Just then, the masked men parted and created a hallway made out of their bodies. A man wearing a ski-mask and black fatigues pushed a wheelchair forth. Another man wearing a ski-mask and black fatigues was seated in the chair. He was holding a machine gun with an infrared laser on it in his black gloved hands. The man pushing him stopped the wheelchair in front of God and La'Quan.

La'Quan was barely conscious having bumped the back of his head on the floor when God had tackled him.

The masked man in the wheelchair reached underneath his chin and peeled off his ski-mask back from over his face, revealing his identity. The man in the mask wasn't a man at all. It was actually a woman. It was Billie. She locked eyes with God and cracked a one-sided smile. He cracked one back at her.

"Hey, my handsome, husband," Billie greeted him. She then looked over her shoulder at the man that had been pushing her wheelchair, saying, "Uncle Kershawn, cut that rope off my hubby, please." She looked at La'Quan. "Then, stand this dick-head up by his friend there." She threw her head toward Marquette who still had his hands in the air.

"This fucking mask is hot as shit!" Kershawn complained as he peeled off his ski-mask off his face and tucked it into his back pocket. He picked up La'Quan's katana and cut God free from the chair.

"Thanks, OG," God said as he patted him on his arm.

"Don't mention it," Kershawn replied and tossed the katana aside. He grabbed La'Quan under his arm and roughly pulled him to his feet. He half dragged and half walked him over to Marquette to stand beside him. He was still a little out of it from bumping the back of his head when he was tackled.

"Thank you, baby," God told Billie, as he hugged and kissed her.

"You're welcome, baby," she replied with a smile, looking at him rubbing and kissing her stomach. He was communicating to their unborn child that he loved it too. "You were right. Those watches came in handy. That's how we were able to find you."

"I figured as much." God smirked and glanced at his

digital watch with the location device installed in it.

"I was gon' have my boys chop 'em down, but I figured you'd like to be the one to do the honors," Kershawn said to God, as he approached him, taking the strap of the machine gun from around his head and handing it to him.

"You know me so well," God told him, as he received the machine gun, examining it and making sure it was fully loaded. He tapped its trigger and activated its infrared laser. He dapped up Kershawn and took a step toward La'Quan and Marquette. He felt Billie smack him on his ass as he proceeded in their direction, mad-dogging them.

God stopped in front of La'Quan and Marquette and lifted up his machine gun. The killaz stood where they were with their hands up and staring him down, fearlessly. He had to tilt his hat to them—they were brave and had nuts the size of King Kong. Although he respected them, that wasn't going to stop him from killing them. They lived by the gun so they'd die by the gun. Straight like that!

Buratatatatatatatatatat!

God narrowed his eyes as he swept his machine gun back and forth across La'Quan and Marquette. They fell to their bloody death and lay on their backs, smoking. Seeing them twitch here and there, he stalked toward them to finish them off. Determination in his eyes and vengeance in his heart, he stood over them, sweeping his machine gun over them again. Their movements ceased, their bodies smoked, their torsos bled, and empty shell casings lay at their feet.

Keeping his eyes on La'Quan and Marquette's dead bodies, God lowered the machine gun at his side. He spoke to everyone inside the warehouse without turning around. "Now, let's catch up with Country and Buck Wild."

Chapter 7

The Mercedes Benz vans ripped up the street, leaving debris in their wake. God was riding shotgun in the van leading the fleet. He was wearing a bullet-proof vest over his shirt that Billie had given him and clutching the machine gun Kershawn had blessed him with. They'd caught up with Country and Buck Wild a way back. They were about to light their asses up, but the cousins caught them making their move and sped off. Now they were in hot pursuit of them.

"There they go, OG, slide up on the driver—I'ma take his ass out first," God told Kershawn who was behind the wheel.

"I gotchu faded," Kershawn said. He dipped into the other lane beside Buck Wild's whip. Seeing they were gaining on their targets, God readjusted himself in the front passenger seat and focused his attention on the side of the windshield the driver of Buck Wild's car was on. He could see Country's silhouette behind the glass. He was the one behind the wheel. Seeing the outlining of Country's head and body caused a wicked smile to stretch across his face.

God let the passenger window down, and the night's cool air rushed inside. The wind ruffled his naturally curly hair and the shirt he wore underneath his bullet-proof vest. He narrowed his eyes into slits, as the air blew hard against his face. He hung halfway out of the window and clutched his machine gun tighter. The van drove side by side with Buck Wild's truck. God aimed his blower at him and pulled its trigger. The deadly weapon vibrated in his hands, and empty shell casings jumped out of the side of it.

Blatatatatatatatat!

The driver's window shattered, and broken glass went flying everywhere. The truck swerved out of control and slammed into a wooden telephone pole. The impact from the SUV crashing shifted the pole in the ground and sent Country imploding out of the windshield. He hit the ground hard, and tumbled even harder. By the time he stopped tumbling, he was lying on his back. His arms and legs were stretched out. There was a huge knot on his forehead, and he was bleeding blackish red blood from out of his scalp. Blood was running out of his nostrils, and his mouth was bloody. His top row of teeth was missing, and he was pretty sure his arm was broken from him landing on it. He lay where he was, moaning in pain. He was covered in broken glass and surrounded by it as well. It all twinkled under the moonlight.

"Awwww, fuck! My mothafucking arm, bruh! My mothafucking arm is broken!" Country hollered in agony, tears dancing in his eyes. He looked at his arm and it was broken, twisted at a funny angle.

The Mercedes Benz vans stopped. God was the first one to hop out, gripping his machine gun and looking around for any potential witnesses. Kershawn and the rest of his masked up men hopped out of the other van. Armed, they started in the same direction as God, but they stopped once he turned to them, raising his hand.

"Y'all niggaz fall back, I got this!" God called out to them. The masked up men stayed where they were, and waited for God to handle his business.

God kept his eyes on Country, as he strolled toward him cool and calm, machine gun at the ready. He had the red dot of his blower shining on the back of Country's head. Once he heard someone approaching him, Country looked to his right and saw the silhouette of a man. He knew he had some sort of semi-automatic weapon with an infrared laser in his hands. Seeing the man in his entirety at the corner of his eye, he realized it was God coming at him, and he was there to take him to Heaven or Hell—whichever one he thought was fit for him.

Country scrambled to his feet and limped down the street as fast as he could, occasionally glancing over his shoulder. God casually pursued him, never breaking his stride to chase him down. He knew that Country was low hanging fruit, and he was easy for the picking. He was positive he'd catch up with him. That's why he was whistling as he went after him; red dot lingering on his left leg.

Buratatatatatat!

God swept his firing machine gun across Country's legs and chopped him down. He plopped belly first to the ground and howled painfully. Wincing, he pulled himself up the road, dragging his mangled legs behind him. When he glanced over his shoulder and saw God still on his trail, he crawled faster, desperately trying to escape his wrath.

"I don't know how much that punk-ass nigga Joaquin paid y'all to flip on me, but I hope it was worth it. I really do 'cause it's most definitely gon' cost you and Buck." God said those words as he continued to stalk Country. He could hear police car sirens heading to his location, but he didn't give a fuck. He wasn't leaving until he'd knocked Country's head off.

"We—we hadda do it, bruh—nigga—nigga kidnapped my girl and my shawty—" Country said painfully. His face was covered in small bloody cuts he'd gotten from flying through the windshield of the truck. He was slobbering and bleeding on the asphalt. "He said if we didn't deliver you to dem niggaz back there that—that—that he was gonna kill 'em both."

God's forehead wrinkled upon hearing Country's explanation of why he and Buck Wild had betrayed him.

"Joaquin is holding Nadine and yo' seed hostage, where at?"

Country winced as he struggled to turn on his side to see God's face. He'd lost a lot of blood and was trying his best to keep from fainting. "It's him and some lil' Mexican fuck by the—by the name of—T—T—Tec, bruh, they've got 'em down in—inside of the basement at—" he went on to give him the address of the house. "You've gotta—gotta get me to a hospital, bruh—I'm—I'm bleeding bad and—and I'm hurt—" he held his palm at his mouth and coughed up slimy blood into it. When he looked up at God, he saw double and his vision blurred. His vision returned to normal, and he saw him pointing his machine gun at him. It was then that he knew he was going to die right then.

"I'ma do my best to get cho family back, dog—You've got my word on that," God told him. "But as far as you and Buck Wild—this is where the road ends for you niggaz. Regardless of the situation, y'all shoulda hollered at me. We coulda worked to figure this shit out together."

"We—we couldn't, bruh. Dude—Dude had us wearing these glasses so he—he could see what we were doing and saying the entire time," Country confessed to him.

God noticed half of the glasses Country was talking about were still on his face. He figured he'd ruined them when he went flying out of the windshield of Buck Wild's truck. Hearing the sound of a helicopter's propeller slicing through the air, God looked far across the sky and saw what he believed was a police helicopter coming his way, shining its spotlight. He then looked back at Country who was looking like he was half dead.

"Still, you know how I get down, my nigga—It's death before dishonor with me," God told him, as he focused the red laser of his machinegun on his chest. "Ezekiel 5:15, *So it shall be a reproach and a taunt, an instruction and an astonishment unto the nations that are round about thee, when I shall execute judgments in thee in anger and in fury and in furious rebukes. I the Lord have spoken it.*" He pulled the trigger of his machine gun, and it vibrated in his hands. Rapid fire spat from its barrel and tore up Country's chest. The back of his head slammed back against the pavement, and God walked up on him. He focused his machine gun on his face and blew his face apart, leaving a bloody mess in the street. His eyes lingered on Country for a minute, as he admired his handiwork. Running back to the Mercedes Benz van, he looked to his left and saw Buck Wild's truck. He saw Buck Wild with a bloody gash in his forehead and his eyeglasses hanging halfway off his face. He was barely conscious and moaning.

Stopping, God pointed his machine gun at him and pulled its trigger. Bullets ripped through the driver's window, shattering it and blowing off the side of his Buck Wild's face. The truck abruptly exploded when the black box device on his collar was struck. The force from the explosion was so powerful it hurled God backwards and blew his machine gun out of his hand. The truck shot straight up into air like it was being launched into space by fire. In midair, it flipped upside down and crashed back down upon its roof, engulfed by flames. The fire from the wrecked SUV cast its golden orange illumination on everything surrounding it, including the Mercedes Benz vans and the masked men occupying them.

God sat up and looked around for his machine gun. Spotting it, he scrambled to his feet and ran over to it, picking it up. He looked into the sky with his hand held over his brows, and saw the police helicopter approaching fast. Holding the machine gun with both hands, he ran back to the Mercedes Benz van as fast as he could and jumped into the front passenger seat. As soon as he slammed the passenger door shut, Kershawn floored the gas pedal and took off like a bat out of hell.

"Yo', this nigga got my man's girl and his seed," God informed Kershawn, as he checked the magazine of his machine gun.

"Who? Joaquin?" Kershawn asked, as he looked back and forth between him and the windshield.

The magazine was halfway full, so God smacked it back into his machine gun. "Yeah, he gave me the address where they're holed up. Said a lil' Mexican nigga and Joaquin has 'em. They were the ones that sent them to snatch me up and drop me off to them two fools back at the warehouse I laid down."

"Now, lemme guess, they did what they did so he wouldn't kill 'em?"

"You guessed it," God said, laying the machine gun in his lap and holding onto the handle hanging from the ceiling on the passenger side.

"Gemme the address so I can program it into the navigation system," Kershawn told him, as he opened up the navigation system on the small screen at the center of the van's dashboard. As God gave him the address where Nadine and the baby were being held, he programmed it into the system. Instantly, a feminine voice spoke telling him how long it was going to take him to reach his destination. He then told him where make a turn, in a certain number of miles.

***

Gun in hand, Aztec sat in a chair across from Nadine, watching her rock her infant son to sleep. He'd occasionally doze off, but pop right back up. He'd been up for the past week, conducting business on Joaquin's behalf; so he was exhausted. Aztec wasn't anyone's fool. He knew as soon as he fell asleep, Nadine was going to make her grand escape; so he had to be alert. Unfortunately for him, he was finding that harder and harder by the second. Eventually, Aztec succumbed to the inevitable and winded up slumped in the chair, snoring.

Nadine, who had been watching him closely, thought he was setting a trap for her ass. She wanted to make her move and flee her homemade prison, but she had to be sure that he was truly asleep. Deciding to test him out, she called out his name and stomped her foot. He didn't say a thing or make a move, so she believed he was knocked out. Sneakily, Nadine strapped the infant carrier to her body and slipped her baby inside of it. She slipped her bare feet out of her heels so she wouldn't make any noise in them while walking across the floor. She then got upon her feet and slowly crept toward the staircase. She'd gotten halfway across the floor when she'd heard the metallic click of the hammer of a gun.

Nadine froze stiff with fear and looked in Aztec's direction. He was mad-dogging her and pointing his gun at her.

"Y adónde diablos crees que vas, perra? (*And just where in the fuck do you think you're going, bitch?*)" Aztec asked threateningly. Nadine swallowed the lump of fear in her throat and lifted her hands in the air, surrendering. Tears twinkling in her eyes, she slowly stepped backwards toward the chair she was seated in.

"Please, please, don't shoot me," Nadine pleaded, as tears slid down her cheeks.

"Sit cho black ass in that chair—now!" Aztec ordered and pointed with his gun.

"Okay, okay, okay." Nadine wiped the tears from her eyes with her fingers and sat down in the chair.

"If you ever pulla stunt like that again, I'll blow yo' brains out, you hear me?"

"Yes, yes, I hear you."

Holding Nadine at gunpoint, Aztec pulled a vial of cocaine out of his pocket that Joaquin had given him some time ago. Now, normally he stuck with weed and stayed the fuck away from hard drugs. But Joaquin had hipped him to the fact that coke could keep a nigga up for days at a time if he tooted enough of it. That was how he'd been able to stay up the entire week. He'd been trying not to snort any more so he could avoid becoming addicted, but the situation he was in called for him to be wide awake. With that in mind, Aztec tapped some of the powdery substance onto his fist and snorted it up his right nostril. The sensation he got was like a punch to the face, and it caused his eyes to water. He felt his nostril threatening to drip, so he snorted again. Afterward, he wiped any white residue from around his nose with the back of his fist, licked it from off his hand and tucked the vial back inside of his pocket.

"Okay, I'm up; I'm really up this time. Whooo!" Aztec smacked his face to hype himself up, even more than the coke had. He jumped up and down and continued to smack himself, pacing the floor. Hearing several doors closing outside in the street, Aztec's forehead wrinkled, and he snatched up a folding chair. He planted it below the basement window and climbed upon it. "I'm finna take a look outta this window, if you try to run, I'ma empty this whole clip in yo' back. You got that?" Nadine nodded *yes*. Aztec peered out of the dirt-smudged basement window. He saw God and Kershawn jogging across the street with machine guns. His eyes widened and his mouth flung open.

He knew they were coming after him, but they wouldn't get him easily.

Niggaz think they're about to come up in here and wet me up and save this bitch? Nah, they got me fucked all the way up. I'ma killa! I'll go out inna blaze behind mine! Straight up, Aztec thought as he jumped down to the floor, hearing God and the goons kicking at the front door upstairs.

"Get up! Get the fuck up!" Aztec hollered at Nadine as he pointed his gun at her. She hopped up to her feet, looking scared as a bitch.

"What's the matter? What's going on?" Nadine asked in a panic, fearing for her and her baby's lives.

Aztec held her at gunpoint, as he unstrapped the infant carrier from her body. "Take it off! Take this shit off so I can put it on!" he demanded, as he took a step back, clutching his gun with both hands and pointing it at her. Crying, Nadine swiftly slipped off the infant carrier and helped Aztec slip it on. He ordered her to strap the infant carrier around his back, and she did. At this time, he could hear God and his goons racing down the staircase. As soon as Nadine finished strapping the infant carrier to his back, Aztec snatched Nadine closer to him and pressed his blower to the back of her dome. He turned her toward the staircase, just as God and his goons reached the landing. Once God and his goons saw Aztec and Nadine, they pointed their machine guns at them. Their infrared laser beams shone on Nadine as well as Aztec's face and whatever else of him was exposed.

"Don't shoot! Please, I beg of you, don't shoot! He—He—He has my—my baby strapped to 'em." Nadine cried aloud, tears pouring down her face and dripping off her chin.

"Hold on, y'all lower y'all straps, that's my man's girl he's using as a human shield!" God said as he lowered his machine gun. The goons didn't lower their machine guns until Kershawn gave the approving nod. "Look, man," he addressed Aztec, "I'm not tripping off you, bruh, the only nigga's head I want is Joaquin's. As soon as you let the girl go and tell me where he is, you can walk—you have my word."

"Suck my dick! I'd never give up my hermano! That's mi familia, homeboy. I don't know where you're from but we obviously aren't cut from the same cloth! I'll never give up big bro! Fuck that and fuck you!" Aztec spat back, heatedly. If there was one thing he believed in, it was loyalty. If he was riding with you, then it was until the wheels fell off. That's how he got down for his!

"You've got quite the mouth on you, son," Kershawn chimed in.

"Oh, yeah? Well, I've got quite the gun too, pops," Aztec said. "The way I look at it, I'm the one with the leverage so I'm the one calling the shots. So, this is how we're gonna play this shit. Y'all gon' throw down your cuetes and lay down with your hands behind your heads. Then, you're gonna gemme a numbre I can reach one of you to get this kid back."

"What? You've got some set of balls on you! Fuck you, man!" one of the goons said.

Blowl!

Nadine's head launched forward as the back of it exploded from the impact of a bullet. Her blood splattered on Aztec's face and the baby. In fact, the child was startled by the loud gunshot, and it started crying. God and the goons looked on in horror at Nadine's body, as it fell lifelessly to the floor, a pool of blood forming around it.

Aztec looked like he'd gone insane after pulling the trigger. His face was contorted with anger, and his chest was heaving up and down. He wiped the blood from his face and left smears of it behind. He placed his gun to the baby's head.

"I'm telling y'all now I'm not one for talking or repeating myself," Aztec said, with regard to why he'd slumped Nadine without hesitation. "Now, either y'all gon' do like the fuck I said, or on my life this baby is getting it next. Fuck with me if you want to!" He looked around at all of the faces in the basement that posed a threat to him.

"You kill the kid and you don't have anything to bargain your way outta here with," another one of the goons said.

"You're right," Aztec admitted and then blew his brains out. His shooting the goon startled everyone like his shooting Nadine did. Now, everyone knew the young bull wasn't a stranger to killing shit and he'd make good on his threats. "Homeboy there is absolutely right about my killing of this lil' one. I honestly wouldn't have a bargaining chip to get outta this basement. But what he doesn't know is I'm hyped up offa coca and don't give a fuck if I make it outta here dead or alive. I'm willing to go out guns blazing, bro." He pulled out a second gun which he pointed at them along with his first one.

For a minute the basement was quiet except for the loud cries of Nadine and Country's infant son. Kershawn, realizing they were in a losing situation, spoke up to control the situation at hand.

"Alright, everyone, throw your guns down and lay on the floor, with your hands behind your heads," Kershawn gave his men strict orders, and they complied. Aztec smiled triumphantly and lowered his guns, stepping over the bodies of Kershawn, God, Billie and the goons—ready to shoot anyone if they dared to make a move. Once he'd finally made it to the staircase, Kershawn called him back and he turned around. "You forgot to get our contact so you can tell us where you're leaving the kid."

"Well, I'm listening, pops," Aztec said.

Kershawn looked to God and nodded. God went on to give Aztec the number to his cellular.

"Alright, I've got it memorized—I'll be in touch," he said before heading out of the basement.

Aztec tucked one of his guns in the front of his jeans once he'd made it upon ground level. He found a cherry red Dodge Charger with two black racing stripes and smashed its driver's window in, with the butt of his gun. The alarm went off loudly. He quickly disarmed it and swept as much of the broken glass off the driver's seat as he could. After he hotwired the vehicle, he plopped down in the seat, fired it up and peeled off. Putting in his blue-tooth, he hit up Joaquin to let him know what had gone down. Joaquin then gave him instructions of the next move he was to make before hanging up.

"Shhhhh—Everything is gonna be okay, lil' man—Uncle Tec isn't gonna hurt chu—I just hadda show those putas how gangsta I was," Aztec told the baby, as he patted his back comfortingly. "It's beena while since you've eaten. I take it you're hungry. You know I read in this magazine while I was locked up that when a baby clenches and unclenches its fists that it means they're hungry. How about we stop atta gas station and I cop you a half a gallon of milk and a baba? Sounds like a plan? Okay, lil' man." Looking up ahead, Aztec saw an AMPM gas station coming up on the right side of the street.

***

The Mercedes Benz van pulled up on a residential block. Its back door came open, and Kershawn jumped down. He reached back for his machine gun, and one of his men passed it to him. He looked up and down the street for the vehicle Aztec had told him he'd left the baby in. He spotted the cherry red Dodge Charger six cars up the block. He motioned his men to follow him, and they moved in on the Charger like they were a SWAT team. Coming upon the car, Kershawn saw the baby inside on the backseat. He was lying on his back with a bottle of milk tilted upon a balled up shirt. He was halfway asleep while he sucked on the bottle's nipple.

Kershawn gave his men the signal to lower their machine guns. He smiled, looking at the baby. "I guess that midget did have a heart—A black one, but stilla heart nonetheless."

Kershawn slipped the strap of the machine gun over his head and opened the back door of the Dodge Charger. He scooped the baby into his arms and held the bottle to his mouth, walking him back toward the Mercedes Benz van, with his men following closely behind him.

***

Joaquin pulled up to the address that Madrid had given him, parked, and killed the engine of his car. Hearing a vehicle approaching from his rear, he glanced at his side view mirror and found a black Mercedes Benz van driving past him. Once it had vanished down the street, he tucked his blower underneath the driver's seat and hopped out of his whip. As soon as he stepped foot upon the curb, God and a half a dozen of men wearing ski-masks ran upon him, machine guns in hand. Hearing them descending upon him, Joaquin turned around to face them.

"Qué pasa ahora, perra? (*What's popping now, bitch?*)"

God spoke what little Spanish he did know with a smirk on his face. "You scared, pussy?"

"Not at all," Joaquin smiled devilishly. "El que teme a la muerte está en negación (*He who fears death is in denial*)."

"Brave man—I'll be sure that quote of yours gets chiseled on your tombstone." God scowled. Having found Humphrey dead and the girls gone, God and Billie set out to find them. Luckily, both of the girls were still wearing the watches he'd given them, with the tracking devices installed in them. That's how they were able to locate them; running into Joaquin was just an added bonus.

"If you're here I take it that you know where the girls are now," Joaquin said. God frowned, wondering how he knew that. "That means yes. You should know that the only way he's letting them walk outta there is if I give myself up."

"He? Who the fuck is he?" God asked curiously.

"That's what I wanna know," Billie said, stepping up behind Joaquin. He glanced over his shoulder at her and turned back around to God.

Joaquin gave them a quick rundown of him and Madrid's history and how he'd contacted him to meet with him. Having been given the pertinent information, God agreed to let Joaquin enter the house that Madrid was holed up with the girls.

"Alright, I'm willing to let chu go in there if it means the girls are gonna walk. But make no mistake—once they're free, we're chopping that ass down." God eyed him. "You holding?" he asked, referring to him holding a gun.

Joaquin shook his head. "Nah, it's in the car. I figure he's gonna pat me down once I'm inside anyway."

God nodded understandingly and told one of the goons to give him their ear-bud, which he passed to Joaquin. He started speaking to Joaquin while he adjusted the ear-bud inside of his ear. "Once you've gotten the girls, you contact me through that ear-piece and we'll come busting in."

"Got chu," Joaquin nodded and turned around. As he walked past Billie he mad-dogged her. "Vieja perra culo escandaloso (*Ol' scandalous ass bitch*)," he said under his breath.

God, Billie and the goons hunched down behind the fence of a neighboring house. They watched Joaquin from where they were hiding. Once he was snatched inside the raggedy house with the boarded up windows and graffiti on it, God and his crew invaded the dirt-patched lawn of the house. They hid within the shadowy areas of the run-down crib and waited for Joaquin to give them the word to move in.

Joaquin rapped on the raggedy door and caused paint chips to fall. A moment later, it was snatched open and Madrid shoved his gun in his face, causing him to lift his hands into the air. Madrid stepped outside and took a scan of the block, making sure no one was with Joaquin. He snatched Joaquin inside of the house which was lit by what looked like one hundred burning candles, in the living room and the kitchen. Holding Joaquin at gunpoint, Madrid slammed the door shut and locked it. He forced Joaquin up against the wall, kicking his legs roughly apart. He then patted him down thoroughly to make sure he wasn't strapped. Once his search didn't produce any weapons, Madrid snatched him around so he would be facing him.

"You wanted me, well, here I am," Joaquin said, looking him square in his eyes.

"How could you, mijo?" Madrid asked, as he cocked his head aside, looking at him like he was trying to understand the meaning behind an action he'd taken in the past.

"How could I what?" Joaquin's brows furrowed.

His posing this question seemed to infuriate Madrid. His face balled up angrily, and he took a step back, pointing his gun in his face. "Don't chu play stupid with me, cabron! You know exactly what the fuck I mean! It's because of your actions that I've been sent here to kill you!" His nostrils flared, and he clenched his jaws, chest heaving up and down. "You broke my heart, mijo. You broke it into one thousand pieces." His eyes welled up with water and streamed down his cheeks. Joaquin was shocked to see his mentor shedding tears. In all of his years of knowing him, he'd never cried. Hell, he rarely showed any emotions at all. In fact, he'd seen him laugh maybe three times in his entire life. It was from this that he knew that killing him, someone he looked at as a son, would hurt him to the core of his soul.

"Lemme guess, Ignacio put it out there that I killed our mother and father, huh?" Joaquin asked. Madrid's lack of response told him that his assumption was true. "I shoulda known, that fucking back-biting serpiente!" His face balled up hatefully, thinking of how much he despised Ignacio. He absentmindedly found himself balling his fists so tight that the veins in them bulged.

"You know what, fuck all of this emotional bullshit, poppa!" Madrid said, getting his mind back in kill-mode again. Swiftly, he wiped the tears from his eyes and clutched his blower tighter, cocking its hammer back. "All I wanna know before I knock your goddamn head off is how could you murder the two people who adopted you into their family and treated you like their blood? I wanna know that right now before I leave you stinking in this shithole so talk—now!"

"Is that what chu wanna know? Huh?" Joaquin asked heatedly.

"Yes, that's what the fuck I wanna know!" Madrid spat

back with a higher octave. He was just as heated as Joaquin was.

"Okay, I killed 'em because—" Joaquin cut himself short. With blinding speed, he smacked Madrid's gun out of his face causing him to instinctively pull its trigger. It fired. Quickly, Joaquin spat a Gemstar razor into his palm. He swung the small razor blade in a downward motion and severed the ligaments in Madrid's fingers, making it impossible for him to hold a gun. Whipping around in a one hundred and eighty degree turn, Joaquin brought the crimson stained Gemstar around again, going across a vein in Madrid's neck. Madrid's eyes bulged, and his mouth flung open. Blood oozed out of his neck, and he smacked his hand over the wounded area. He staggered backwards and fell to the floor dramatically, knocking over several candles. As he lay on the carpeted floor, two rats scurried past him.

Joaquin walked over to him and kneeled down, showing him the proper way to apply pressure to his bleeding neck. "You just keep applying pressure to it like I showed you. You'll be okay 'til I'm able to get chu some medical attention." He sighed. "For the record, I didn't kill my parents. Never in a thousand years could I bring myself to do such a thing. I loved them more than life itself." Joaquin's eyes became glassy, thinking of his deceased parents. He truly loved and missed them with all of his heart. "Truthfully, it was Ignacio that murdered them." When he said this, Madrid looked at him with disbelief. "Yes. It's true. Ignacio was jealous of my relationship with them and he wanted to be the big boss of Blood Brothers. That day when I came home after we successfully took out Eduardo Maldonado and his soldados, I saw Ignacio murder them in cold blood—" Joaquin went on to tell Madrid what happened that day at Mateo's villa, and his escape to America.

Chapter 8

When Madrid thought about the bombshell Joaquin had dropped on him, it made a lot of sense to him. Ignacio had always expressed how much he despised Joaquin and bragged about how he'd run the cartel once he was boss. He could definitely see his pretty ass making such a bold move against his old man, and shifting the blame to Joaquin.

"I'm—I'm sorry, mijo, I—I didn't know," Madrid apologized as he held Joaquin's hand, looking him in his eyes.

"It's okay, old man. I understand." Joaquin nodded understandingly. "We're soldados and soldados just follow orders." Madrid slightly nodded, happy that Joaquin understood his position. "Now, where are the girls?"

Madrid pulled out a small key from his pocket and gave it to Joaquin. "They're—they're inside of the—the bathroom—that's—that's the key to open the padlock."

"Okay, hang tight—I'll be right back," Joaquin told him before he stood upright. He entered the hallway and looked around for the bathroom door. Spotting a door with a padlock on it, he darted down the hallway and used the key to open the lock. Once he'd unlocked the padlock, he quickly removed it and tossed it aside.

Joaquin tried to open the door, but it didn't budge. He slammed his shoulder against it three times before it flung open, making a loud—*boom*! The sound resonated throughout the bathroom, causing rats to scatter in disarray. The bathroom was filthy and smelled of feces and urine, which nearly caused Joaquin to vomit. Like the living room and kitchen, it was lit by white candles which cast shadows on the walls. There were black and brown roaches crawling on the walls, sink, toilet, and even the ceiling.

Charity and Annabelle were gagged with bandanas, and their wrists were bound by rope. By Charity's glassy pink eyes and the dried white tears on her face, Joaquin could tell that she'd been crying. Oddly enough, Annabelle didn't look like she'd shed so much as a tear during the entire ordeal. Joaquin rushed over to the tub and removed the gags from out of their mouths.

"Daddy, I knew you'd come and save us. I knew you would!" Annabelle said excitedly, as her father untied the rope that bound her wrists together. Once her wrists were free, she kissed her father and hugged him tightly. "I love you. I love you so much. You love me too right?"

"Are you kidding? I love my baby forever and ever." Joaquin kissed her on the side of her face and rubbed her back affectionately. "Okay. I've got the girls!" he informed God and his crew through his ear-bud. He then untied the rope from around Charity's wrists and helped her out of the tub. He hoisted Annabelle up in his arms, took Charity by her hand and led them out into the hallway. As they neared the living room, they could hear the front door rattling from God and the goons trying to kick it in. By the time Joaquin and the girls entered the living room, the front door flew open. God, Billie, Kershawn and the goons spilled inside. At this time, Madrid had pulled himself up on the wall while holding his wounded neck.

"Daddyyyyyy!" Charity's eyes lit up when she saw her father. She ran over to him, and he picked her up in his arms, hugging her lovingly. He kissed her on the cheek and asked her if she was okay. She told him *yes*.

"Here," God told Billie as he passed her Charity. "Take the girls and wait for us outside."

Billie nodded and looked to Annabelle. "Come on, baby. Let's go."

Annabelle frowned and stepped behind her father, holding him tightly. "No—I'm staying right here with daddy!" she spat defiantly.

"Pretty girl, I'm not gon' play this game witchu—Get your tail over here, now!" Billie said angrily. One crutch was under one arm while she held Charity in her other arm. Her leg was bent at the knee to avoid putting pressure on her ankle.

"No!" Annabelle shouted. "You think I'm stupid, huh? You're gonna let Kyree kill daddy as soon as I leave! But I won't let chu, I won't! You'll have to kill us both! I'd rather die than be without 'em!" Her eyes danced with tears which spilled down her cheeks. Her nostrils flared, and her chest heaved. She was really angry, anxious and upset.

"No one is going to kill your father, baby—I promise—Tell her, Joaquin," Billie said and looked him in his eyes. They both knew that she was full of shit, and that—more than likely—God and his goons planned on gunning him down. Still, if he was to be murdered in cold blood, Joaquin didn't want his baby girl to witness something so traumatizing. Seeing some shit like that would leave her psychologically scarred for life.

Joaquin kneeled down to Annabelle and cupped her face, looking into her eyes. "Pretty girl, I want chu to go along with your mother."

"But, papi, if I do he'll kill you. Kyree and mommy want you dead. And I don't want you to die; I don't want you to die—" Annabelle broke down sobbing, tears spilling down her cheeks. She hugged her father around his neck, and he held on to her, rubbing her back comfortingly.

"I'm not gonna die, pretty girl. I'm not gonna allow anyone or anything in this world to take me away from you."

"You promise?" Annabelle said, looking into his eyes.

"Yes—I promise, baby," Joaquin replied. She extended her pinky, and he hooked his with it, making a pinky swear. "Go ahead now, baby. We'll talk later." He kissed her on the cheek and patted her on her butt playfully as she walked away. "I love you," he called out to her as she followed her mother and Charity out the door.

"I love you, too!" Annabelle replied, as they disappeared through the door.

Joaquin stood upright beside Madrid. They both stared down at God and the goons he had with them. God and the goons pointed their machine guns at them. Joaquin and Madrid held their heads up high and stuck their chests out, prepared to meet their deaths like the brave men they'd portrayed.

"Any last words?" God asked them before he gave the goons the signal to open fire.

"You send my brother to hell and this bitch will be following right behind 'em!" a voice rang out from the kitchen. When God and the goons looked to the kitchen, Aztec walked out with Ms. Jones held at gunpoint. Her mouth was gagged, and her wrists were bound behind her back. She looked terrified, and everyone could tell she'd been crying.

"Ms. Jones!" God said her name aloud. He was surprised to see her. The entire time she'd been gone, he was wondering where she'd disappeared to—and now here she was.

"You really needa step yo' game up, bro, you've been on the losing end all goddamn night," Aztec told God seriously. Joaquin had told Aztec to snatch up Ms. Jones from the super lab and bring her to the current location. He knew he'd eventually run into God sooner or later, and he wanted to have something in his pocket to bargain with.

God looked at Joaquin, and a grin formed at the corner of his lips. It was then that he knew that Joaquin had made the move so that the situation would be in his favor. "Well played, Mr. Torres. Well played."

"I promised my daughter I was leaving out this bitch alive," Joaquin finally spoke up. "That was a promise I wouldn't break even if the fate of the world depended onnit. Having a daughter yourself I'm sure you understand where I'm coming from." God nodded understandingly. "Here's what's gonna happen: my people and I are gonna take the back door outta here, with this old broad. Once we're safely in our vehicle then we'll let her go."

"You ain't even gotta go through alla that, homie, just leave her here and be on your way," God told him.

Joaquin stepped closer to God, looking him dead in his eyes. "Mothafucka, you aren't calling any shots around here! I'm the H.N.I.C in this bitch and I'm telling you how it's rocking. You got that?" God didn't say a word, which infuriated him. "Tec, nod that old bitch!"

"Wait, wait, wait," God said, holding up his hands in a non-threatening manner. "I got it! I got it, okay? You win, bruh. You're the head-nigga-in-charge."

"That's more like it," Joaquin said, looking him up and down like he wasn't shit. "Madrid, Tec, let's roll up outta here."

"After y'all, I'm parked inside of the alley out back," Aztec said, still holding Ms. Jones at gunpoint. He tossed Joaquin his car keys and waited until him and Madrid was outside. Once he heard one of them honking the horn, he smiled and winked at God before easing out of the backdoor. "Don't follow me out! You'll get this cracked-out bitch back once we're gone. I'll have bro honk the horn."

Three minutes had passed once Aztec and Ms. Jones

were gone. As soon as God and the goons heard a horn being honked, they went charging out the back of the house. They saw Ms. Jones sitting down in the alley with the headlights of a gray box Chevy shone on her. They chased after her as the Chevrolet backed up in reverse hastily, leaving a dust cloud in its wake.

God and the goons ran out of the gates. He tended to Ms. Jones while they sent a hail of bullets in the box Chevy's direction, all of which missed it. The Chevrolet swung out into the street and sped off in the opposite direction. The goons lowered their machine guns and approached God. He was kneeling down close to Ms. Jones. He removed her gag and pulled out a butterfly knife. Left, right, up, down and the blade appeared. He used it to cut off the duct tape that bound Ms. Jones' wrists. As soon as she was out of her restraints, she hugged God and broke down sobbing, staining his shirt with her tears.

"It's okay, Ms. Jones. Everything is gonna be all right now." God rubbed her back soothingly. "I got chu. You're safe."

"Oh, thank you, Kyree. Thank you so much for saving me, baby boy." Ms. Jones cried and sniffled as God pulled her up to her feet.

"We'd better get the fuck outta here now—The Boys will be here any minute now that those shots have been fired," God told the goons. His cellular chimed with a message. He looked at it. It was Billie.

Billie: *Heard gunshots, r u good?*

God: *I'm str8, ma. Head back to the house. I'll be there shortly.*

Billie: *K. Love U.*

God: *Love U 2.*

God slipped his cellular back in his pocket and held Ms.

Jones close to him, as he walked her out of the alley. The goons brought up their rear, making sure they were safely guarded. Shortly thereafter, their Mercedes Benz van pulled up at the end of the alley, and another goon jumped down. He was masked up and clutching a machine gun. His neck was on a swivel as he watched everything around him. By this time, police car sirens could be heard far in the distance heading to that very location.

"Ky—Kyree, listen, I know—I know this isn't the right time to be asking you this, baby—But—But I—I—I need me a fix, baby—I'm feeling sick—I mean, really, really sick," Ms. Jones told him shamefully. She was embarrassed to ask him for crack, but she knew he'd understand her position. After all, he was a crack dealer so he knew how fucked up a fiend could be if they didn't get their usual high.

"It's okay, Ms. Jones—I'ma take good care of you—Real good care of you," God said, as he helped Ms. Jones inside of the Mercedes Benz van. He climbed inside of the van behind her and closed the door. He gave the driver the word to drive off, and he obliged him.

God pulled out his cellular and hit up one of his workers. He told him in coded words to drop off a few grams to Ms. Jones' house.

***

God leaned his head back and he held his dick, pissing into the toilet. Once he'd finished relieving himself, he wagged the urine dripping from his pee-hole and zipped his piece back up. After he let down the lid, he flushed and washed his hand at the porcelain sink. He splashed some cool water on his face and looked up at his reflection in the medicine cabinet mirror.

While Ms. Jones was busy smoking crack in her bedroom, God and the nigga he'd asked to drop off the work for Ms. Jones cleaned up the mess that was made during Aztec's invasion of her home. After they were done, they smoked a blunt and chit-chatted for a while. God threw him a few dollars for his troubles, and the nigga offered to kick it for a while to watch his back, but God insisted he was good and sent him on his way.

God had been through a hell of a lot those past couple months, and he was surprised he'd survived it all. He should have been dead, but through the grace of his namesake he prevailed. The crazy part about it was, the beef between him and Joaquin was far from over. And it never would be until one of them was worm and maggot food.

God took a deep breath and patted his face dry on one of the towels on the rack. He dried off his hands, and left the bathroom, pulling the door shut behind him. He journeyed down the hallway to Ms. Jones' bedroom door and rapped on it. He waited for her to answer, but she never responded. He opened the door to tell her he was leaving, and was instantly slapped in the face by the overwhelming smell of burning plastic. The smell was actually crack! Ms. Jones was lying across the bed asleep, still clutching her old, beat-up crack pipe in her hand. Lying not too far beside her was a blue Bic lighter.

A smirk formed at the corner of God's lips, while looking at Ms. Jones. He was happy that he was able to get her back. Had something happened to her, he would have been devastated. She'd told him how she'd been kidnapped and forced to cook crack inside a lab. She also told him about all of the other crackfiends that Joaquin had working there, as well as the armed guards he had on deck. In his heart God felt that it was his fault that Ms. Jones had been kidnapped. If he hadn't had her cooking up his drugs for him and enabling her by serving her crack, then she'd never had been snatched up. This night he vowed to the Heavenly Father that he was going to get Ms. Jones some help to kick her habit.

How can a nigga say he looks at chu like you his mother but he was serving you crack? Fuck kinda son did I call myself? God thought as he shook his head shamefully. *I promise I'ma do right by you though, ma. I'ma make sure you get clean and live a very fulfilling life. My family and I need you. In fact, we aren't mucha family without chu.*

God grabbed a folded blanket out of the hallway closet and returned to Ms. Jones' bedroom. He sat her crack pipe and her lighter upon the nightstand. He draped the blanket over her and kissed her tenderly on the side of her head, telling her he loved her. Turning off the light, he left her bedroom, pulling the door behind him. God made his way through the living room and unlocked the front door. As soon as he pulled it open, he was startled to find someone there. He reached for his waistline but stopped short when Kershawn stepped from out of the shadowy area of the porch.

"Yo', I almost blasted yo' ass, OG. What's up, though?" God asked, concerned. The first thing he thought was, something had happened to Billie or the girls. If so, he was about to go crazy murking everything in the city.

"They got 'em," Kershawn's voice cracked emotionally, with glassy eyes. "They fucking got 'em, man. Goddamn!" he bit down on his bottom lip and slammed his fist into the doorway angrily.

"Who are you talking about?" God asked, as he pulled him inside of the living room and shut the door. "You know what, hold that thought for a sec. Ms. Jones has a few beers in the fridge, I'ma grab us one."

Kershawn plopped down on the couch and bowed his head, wiping away the wetness in his eyes. He'd always prided himself on being a strong man mentally and physically, so he wasn't trying to break down in front of God. Once he felt like he'd composed himself, he looked back up, and God was returning to the living room, with two bottles of Heineken. He passed one of the green bottles to him and sat down on the arm of the couch.

Kershawn took a long drink from the bottle and wiped his mouth. Normally, he didn't drink any kind of alcohol, but due to the circumstances he was making an exception. "Humphrey. The girls told me that Madrid was the one that killed 'em, man. When we got back to yo' crib we found 'em battered, beaten and bloody, with the back of his fucking head blown out." He showed God with one of his hands how the back of Humphrey's head was missing.

"Where are Billie and the girls?" God asked.

Kershawn swallowed his beer before responding. "I brought 'em along with me. They're outside in my car, don't worry—my joint is bullet-proof and Billie's holding. I only came here to give you the news in person, and avoid that niece of mine from seeing me going to pieces." He took a swig of his beer. "I've been the pillar of strength since her parents died and I've been taking care of the girl. I'm too goddamn prideful to let her see me like this. You know what I mean?"

"I know exactly what you mean," God nodded. "As men we go through shit too, only we keep it all bottled up inside 'cause the world doesn't give a fuck about how we feel. Well, that and the fact that we don't want to appear weak to our peers or our women."

"Amen to that shit," Kershawn said as he leaned forward

and clinked bottles with God. They then took a swig.

"Y'all call the cops?" God inquired.

"Yeah, they came by snooping around and asking a shit load of questions. You know how they do. Billie and I stuck to our usual 'I don't know shit' script. After they left, we jetted over here. I left a couple of my guys at the house to clean up that mess your boy left behind." He spoke of the bloody mess Humphrey's murderer left in his wake. Right then, his cell phone rang and he answered it, placing it to his ear. It was Billie. "What's up, girl? Yeah, we're alright. I'm just helping your newly wedded husband with a few things before we raise up outta here." He made eye contact with God and pretended to smoke a blunt. God nodded understandingly. "Okay, I'll be out there inna minute." He disconnected the call and tossed his cellular on the couch beside him.

"Look, OG, I don't have any loud on me, but I done blew stupid trees over here," God said as he looked around for any ashtrays that may have one of his blunt roaches in it. "So I know I should have a roach end of a blunt or two lying somewhere around here in one of these ashtrays. There it go." He smiled, spotting one of his roaches in an ashtray among many cigarette butts. He got up to retrieve one of them.

"Good," Kershawn said, as he sat his beer down on the coffee table. "I just needa getta lil' buzz going to get my mind right, man. It's been one hell of a night." God approached him with the roach held in his mouth, lighting it, with his hand cupped around it. He took two puffs off it and gave it to Kershawn.

"That's all you," God told him before blowing out a cloud of smoke.

"Good looking out," Kershawn said as he indulged in

the roach, smoke wafting around him. "I'll tell you two things I know for certain. One, it was that old Mexican fuck that took Humphrey out the game. Two, I don't give damn where he goes, I'ma track his ass down and put one in his thinker." He swore with glassy, hurt-filled eyes, tapping his finger against his temple.

"No doubt," God nodded. "And rest assured I'll be right alongside you. We're gone take him and that bitch-ass nigga Joaquin out—once and for all."

Kershawn leaned forward and touched fists with God. They chopped it up until he finished what was left of the blunt, and then Kershawn left the house.

***

The warm morning sunlight shone on God's face, as his eyelids twitched and he smacked his lips. Frowning, he peeled his eyelids open and looked around, confused as to where he was. His forehead creased when he noticed Billie wasn't in bed beside him. He was alarmed once he saw his wife beater and boxer briefs were stained in blood. Looking at his hands, he saw that they were bloody and he was even clutching a bloodstained box-cutter. He tossed the box-cutter aside and grabbed his gun from underneath his pillow. After making sure he had a fully loaded magazine, he smacked it back in and chambered a hollow tip round into it. He hopped upon his bare feet, clutching his gun with both hands and strategically moving out of the bedroom.

"Billie? Billie, are you okay?" God called out as he crossed the threshold into the hallway. Feeling something wet beneath his feet, he looked down to find the carpeted floor soaked and wet. He looked to the bathroom door and saw water pouring out from underneath its door. Cautiously, he approached the bathroom door and flung it open, keeping his back against the side of the doorway. He poked his head inside the bathroom and got a glimpse of someone in the tub.

God swung out into the doorway with his gun up. He saw Billie sitting inside of the tub looking right at him; eyes bulged and mouth hanging open. Her eyes were cloudy. Her complexion was powder blue, and her lips were purple. Her throat had been slashed, and the blood that had poured out of it had dried. The tub of water was tinted pink but constantly overflowing as the faucet was still on. There was also a broken wine glass lying beside the tub, with traces of red wine still inside of it.

"Oh, baby, no, no, no!" God's eyes watered, and tears spilled down his cheeks. He lowered his gun and ran inside the bathroom, slipping and falling. The side of his head ricocheted off the floor, and blood seeped out of it, tinting the water a bright red. His eyes rolled into the back of his head as he blinked his eyelids repeatedly, trying to stay conscious. He sat up where he'd fallen and took the time to gather himself. He crawled over to the bath tub and sat his gun upon its ledge. He then twisted the dial, turning off the water. On his knees, he scooped Billie out of the water and pulled her naked body into him. He kissed her on her forehead as he cried, rocking back and forth. "That nigga Joaquin is dead for doing this, baby! So help me god, I'ma body that nigga and everything he loves!"

God stayed with Billie for three more minutes before laying her flat on the floor. He shut her eyelids, kissed her forehead, and draped towels over her face and body. He grabbed his gun and exited the bathroom, pulling the door shut behind him. As soon as the door clicked closed, he saw one of the girls lying on the bottom bunk limp and bloody, hand dripping on the floor.

God squeezed his eyelids shut and bowed his head. "Heavenly Father, I know I've been one of your greatest sinners, but oh, please, please, Lord—" Tears poured down his cheeks and he sniffled, trying to stop the snot from sliding out of his nostrils. "I beg of you—don't let—don't let that be my baby in that bed. Don't let that be my sweet, sweet, sweet darling Charity." He pleaded with his hands together in prayer, still holding his gun. Wiping his dripping eyes with the hand that held his blower, he composed himself as best as he could before opening the door to Charity and Annabelle's bedroom. As soon as he saw that it was Charity lying on the bottom bunk with her arm and leg hanging off of it, he completely lost it.

"Nooooooo! Oh, gawd, noooooo! Charrrriiiityyyyy, Charrrriiiityyyy!" God threw his head back, screaming over and over again. More tears flowed, and snot oozed out of his nose non-stop, hanging in slimy ropes from the bottom of his chin. Dropping his gun, he dropped down to his knees and bowed his head to the floor. His shoulders shook, as he sobbed uncontrollably and slammed his fist against the floor, pounding it mercilessly. He stayed in this position for a while and then he took a breath, lifting his forehead from the carpet. His eyes were pink and his face was wet and slimy.

Standing over a lifeless Charity, God noticed she'd had her throat and both of her wrists slashed open. Her eyes were cloudy, and her skin had taken on a powder blue complexion. He kneeled down to his baby girl, hugging her around her neck and kissing her on the side of her face and temple. Shutting his eyelids, he prayed to the Almighty. He told him to allow his baby girl into Heaven and watch over her like he would his own. After kissing Charity again, he grabbed her blanket and draped it over her entire body. Looking upon the top bunk, he noticed that Annabelle was gone. He looked around the bedroom from where he stood, but he didn't see her. That's when he heard someone pounding at the front door.

"Police, open up!" a demanding voice said from the other side of the door.

The pounding stopped, but the cops were impatient so it started back up again. Then God's cellular started ringing as he journeyed out of the girls' bedroom and into the hallway. His cellular stopped ringing and then it started ringing again, like someone was desperately trying to reach him.

"Open up or we'll be forced to break down the door!" the demanding voice gave a stern warning. The pounding at the door started right back up again.

Once more God's cellular stopped ringing and started right back up again.

God walked down the hallway, hearing the sound of the television set getting louder the closer he came to the living room. He saw the side of Kershawn's face, as he was focused on the screen. Last night God could tell he was still fucked up about Humphrey, so he invited him to crash on the couch. God and Billie spent nearly the rest of night conversing with him over bottles of brew.

"OG? OG?" God called to him, wearing a frown. He moved counter clockwise around the couch, taking more and more of him in the closer he came to him.

Damn, niggaz got chu too, God thought, shaking his head in pity for him. *You've always beena standup nigga, dog. I was giving your grieving of Humphrey as my reason behind wanting you to crash here last night. But I could tell you knew I really wanted you to stay so I'd have someone here to watch my back in case Joaquin came after my family again.* He crossed himself in the sign of the crucifix.

"Okay, that's it! Break this motherfucker down!" the

demanding voice ordered the other officers.

Boom, boom, boom!

The front door rattled intensely as the police officers were trying to get inside of the house.

Stopping in front of Kershawn, God saw him up close and personal. His eyes were wide and full of horror, and his mouth was stuck open. His eyes were cloudy, and his skin complexion was blue just like Charity's. He was wearing a white V-neck T-shirt and a pair of colorful plaid pajama pants God had lent him to wear for his stay overnight. His throat had been slashed from ear to ear. The blood that had spilled out of his grotesque wound stained the collar of his shirt red.

"Fuck, OG! Bitch-ass nigga got chu too, huh?" God said, as he shook his head in shame for Kershawn. Bowing his head, he crossed himself in the sign of the crucifix. As soon as he brought his head back up—*Boom*!—the front door flew open, sending splinters flying across the living room and startling God. A total of six police officers wearing shiny shields pulled their guns from their holsters and pointed them at him, threateningly. Their faces were pink and angry. Most of them were wearing black sunglasses to combat the sunlight, sporting shaved heads or crew cuts as hairstyles.

"Drop the gun, drop the gun right goddamn now, or I swear to Jesus Christ I'll blow your ass away!" one of the shaved head police officers wearing black sunglasses ordered, with an itchy trigger finger, ready to kill. He was the man behind the demanding voice that was behind the front door.

God dropped the gun. He tried to explain himself, but the Los Angeles' finest weren't trying to hear shit he had to say. As far as they were concerned, he was a black man at the scene of the crime with a fucking gun in his hand. That made him as guilty as sin! "Now, put your hands behind your head and get down on your knees." God complied. "Edwards, cuff 'em!" The commanding officer looked to Officer Edwards and nodded towards God. Officer Edwards holstered his gun and pulled out his handcuffs, walking over to God to cuff his ass up.

"Oh, god, captain, look at this!" one of the police officers said, staring at someone inside the hallway. All of the officers, including the commanding one, looked down the corridor. They saw Annabelle crying with a snotty nose. Her clothes were bloody, and she was holding her side, limping toward them.

"He killed 'em! He killed 'em all! My stepsister, my uncle and my mommy!" Annabelle told the cops and broke down sobbing. "He killed all of 'em and he tried to kill me but I ran and hid!" she confessed. One of the cops rushed over to Annabelle and lifted up her shirt, seeing a bloody wound on her side.

"What happened, honey? You can tell me. You don't have to worry about him." A third police officer scooped Annabelle up into his arm, treating her like the beautiful and gentle flower he believed her to be.

"Owens and the rest of you, checkout the rest of the house, see if there're any survivors!" the captain commanded.

"Okay, captain." Owens motioned for the rest of the cops to follow him. Guns drawn, they combed over the rest of the house and reported two other dead bodies besides Kershawn.

"What did you see?" the captain asked a teary eyed police officer who happened to be an African American man. He wore his hair in a fade and had a goatee. His six-foot-two athletic physique filled out his black uniform, and the sleeves of his shirt hugged his huge biceps.

"There's a woman inside of the bathroom—lying—lying on the floor with her throat slit," the six-foot-two brother reported, as his voice cracked emotionally, and he blinked back tears. "Then—then there's a—a little girl about four or five—years—years old. He slit her throat, cap. That evil son of a bitch slit her wrists and her throat!" He turned his hateful eyes on God who had his wrists handcuffed behind his back. There were two police officers flanking him, holding either of his arms. "You fucking monster!—" the tall brother charged at God like a raging bull. Furious, he gave the kingpin body shots and a right-hook across his jaw. The wicked blow busted God's mouth. The police officers held him up, as he attempted to drop to the floor, his eyes rolled to their whites. The brother wasn't through with him yet, though. "I'll kill you, you mothafucka!" he shouted hysterically and drew down on God. He was just about to put a bullet in his head, but several of the police officers rushed him, leveling his gun up to the ceiling. The shot went wild and crashed into the ceiling, causing debris to trickle down. One of the officers was able to wrestle the gun out of his hands. Crying with snotty nose, the brother tried to break the hold of several police officers and a couple of detectives. He was already a strong man, but the adrenaline added to his strength. He nearly broke their hold twice, but they were able to hold fast.

The brother dropped down to his knees and bowed his head. His entire body shook, as he cried his eyes out, big teardrops splashing on the carpeted floor. The police officers and the detectives continued to hold onto him as he had his mental break down. At this time, the E.M.T's were entering the house with a plastic stretcher and medical supplies. The police officer holding Annabelle passed her to one of the E.M.T's, and they laid her down on the stretcher. They went right to work, lifting up her shirt and cleaning her wound so they could dress it up until she made it to the hospital to get the proper medical attention.

"It's okay, baby girl, everything is going to be alright," one of the E.M.T's assured her. He was a twenty-something white kid with hazel green eyes and long fire engine red hair he wore shaved on the sides and in a bun. "I'm Damien and this is Tory." He motioned to his partner. Tory was a hazelnut-complexioned sister who wore a crown of blonde curly hair, with black highlights.

"Hi, lil' mama," Tory smiled at Annabelle, and waved to her in a friendly manner. "No need to be afraid, we're gonna see to it that you get all the help you need, okay?"

Annabelle heard Damien and Tory, but her attention was focused on God. She was silently crying, and she had a mustache of transparent green snot above her top lip. The E.M.T's exchanged concerned glances, looking at God who was spitting blood on the floor, as the police officers were pulling him back up to his feet, and then back at Annabelle. She hadn't taken her eyes off of him, and she was trembling fearfully. Her bottom lip shook, and a fresh set of tears clouded her eyesight before coating her cheeks.

"What's wrong, lil' mama, you can tell me." Tory told Annabelle seriously.

"Him—he—he killed 'em all—" Annabelle broke down, sobbing and pointing at God accusingly. "He killed my mommy, my uncle and my stepsister—and—and—he promised to kill me—too." She wailed and started crying again. Tory hugged her to her bosom and rubbed her back, trying to console her.

"She's lying, she's fucking lying! That lil' bitch is

fucking lying!" God yelled repeatedly, fighting against the police officers as they struggled to get him out of the house. "You lil' fucking whore, you did this! You and your fucking father! You guys did this!" He harped up mucus and spat it at her, but it missed, landing on Tory's pants. God nearly snatched away from the police officers, as he kicked in Annabelle's direction. He turned to one of the arresting police officers. "That lil' demonic whore and her fucking father did this! I swear! I fucking swear to you, they're the real killaz! They are the real killaaaaz!" God's voice trailed out of the house, as he was escorted down the steps. He was shoved into the back of a police car, and the door was slammed on him. His head popped back up in the back-passenger window. Hysterical, he slammed his forehead against the window as hard as he could, until he opened a bloody gash in it. He then spat on the window and screamed into it. "I'll get you for this, you hear me, goddamn! I'll fucking get you for thiiiiis!" His hot breathed fogged up the back-passenger window. Abruptly, the police car drove away.

Chapter 9

Sunset

The homicide detectives back at God's house had questioned Annabelle and let the ambulance take her to the nearest hospital where she was given stitches. She was also given over-the-counter medication to sooth her pain. The entire time, Joaquin had been there by her side. One of the investigating detectives had gotten a hold of him to tell him what happened and what hospital Annabelle was being taken for medical attention. They'd been at the hospital a total of three and a half hours when Annabelle was finally given discharge paperwork and released.

The automatic double glass doors of the hospital's entrance slid apart, as Joaquin emerged with Annabelle by his side. She had a thin blue hospital blanket wrapped around her shoulders, and she was sucking on a lollipop one of the medical staff had given her. Joaquin handed the valet his ticket for him to recover his whip. He watched as the valet read off the ticket number to his co-worker over the walkie-talkie, so he'd know what vehicle to bring up. As the valet had radioed in what car was to be fetched, he busied himself with his Galaxy cell phone, scrolling through Instagram. Joaquin and Annabelle sat beside each other on the bench, waiting for their car. Smiling, he hugged his little girl into him and kissed her on top of her head while she sucked on her lollipop.

"How are you feeling, pretty girl?" Joaquin asked her.

"I'm okay, papi, the medicine they gave me is working," Annabelle replied.

"Well, you lemme know if you need any more 'cause I've got more," he told her, holding up the white bag with the blue RX logo on it.

"Alright. Can I see your cell phone so I can play games onnit?"

"What happened to the one I gave you?"

"You told me to make sure I get rid of it, remember?"

"I remember." He smiled at her, as he played with her hair. "I was just testing you to make sure you did like I asked."

"You're always testing me, daddy. I told you notta worry about a thing. I got us." She took his cellular from him and started up the game she wanted to play.

"True," he replied and hung his arm around her neck, affectionately. She kissed him on his hand and continued to play her game. "I'm so proud of you, you know that? You did a fantastic job."

"Thank you, papi."

"You don't regret completing your mission, do you?"

"No—I love you—I want you in my life forever and ever," she said confidently, as she continued to play the game. "Kyree, Billie and Annabelle were going to kill you. So, I did what chu told me was a 'necessary evil'."

"That's right, pretty girl, it was most definitely a necessary evil," Joaquin told her. He hated to have put his daughter in the position that he had, but he felt like what he did was completely necessary. All of the other attempts he'd made on God's life weren't successful. So he figured the only way he was going to get that nigga out of his hair was to have someone on the inside get him. That's when he came up with the plan to have Annabelle kill her family while they slept. Her mother had gotten into the habit of being asleep all day and up into the wee hours of the morning. She liked to have a glass of red wine while she relaxed in a hot bubble bath. That's why Annabelle was sure to slip her a couple of

Ambien into the bottle she'd poured from. Then when she'd fallen asleep, she slit her throat without remorse. Joaquin had her knock off Kershawn too. He reasoned that the old head wasn't stupid, and he'd eventually find out it was him behind the intricate plot. And when he did he'd come after him with everything he had to make sure he was dead.

"I love you, pretty girl," Joaquin told her, as he watched her play the game on his cell phone.

"I love you so much more, papi. Kisses?" Annabelle puckered her lips up at him. He gave her a smooch and rubbed her arm, as they continued to wait for his car to arrive.

"Here's our ride. Come on." Joaquin grabbed hold of Annabelle's hand and rose from the bench, walking to the curb to receive his car.

"Papi, where's Uncle Tec?" Annabelle asked curiously.

"He's taking care of something for me, baby," Joaquin told her, as he pulled a ten dollar bill out of his pocket and passed it to the guy who'd brought his car to him. The guy thanked him, as he handed him his car keys. He hopped into his car, made sure Annabelle's seatbelt was secured around her, and then he drove off. Annabelle found an old Beyonce song on the radio. She sang along with the talented vocalist, and danced in her seat. Joaquin looked at her and smiled. He focused his attention back on the road ahead, and his thoughts drifted off to Murtaugh and Hugo. He knew for sure Hugo was dead because he'd gotten the call from his people to let him know about his demise. And he was positive Murtaugh had gotten the business on the account of God's bitch-ass answering his cell phone and telling him he'd missed.

Rest in peace to my niggaz, man, if it wasn't for them I couldn't have built my empire. I'ma make sure y'all have legendary funerals and that your familias are financially taken care of. I swear on the lives of my parents, Joaquin thought as he turned off the grounds of the hospital and entered the flow of traffic, flying down the road.

***

Ms. Jones stirred awake, blinking her eyes rapidly and looking around. She didn't know where she was at first, but then her vision came into focus as she realized she was inside her bedroom. She looked to her nightstand and saw her crack pipe and Bic lighter lying upon it. She sat up and brought her legs over the edge of the bed. When she looked to the mirror on her dresser, she could see the reflection of her bedroom window, which had curtains draped over it. There was very little sunlight shining through the slight opening of the curtains, so she knew it had to have been the butt-crack of dawn.

"Well, I can't start the day without eating," Ms. Jones said to no one in particular, sticking her crack pipe in her mouth and grabbing her lighter. "Breakfast is the most important meal of the day." She struck the metal ball of the lighter with her thumb, and a blue flame sprung upward. She held the fire to the tip of the glass dick and sucked on the end of it, pulling the smoke into her lungs. After getting higher than the law should allow, Ms. Jones sat her glass stem and lighter down upon the nightstand. She then stripped down to her dingy bra and panties, and put on a fresh outfit. She was about to hit the streets to gather up whatever she could to turn in for a profit.

Ms. Jones opened her closet door and pulled out a wooden baseball bat with straight and bent nails embedded in it. She shut the closet door and hoisted the baseball bat up.

Holding it with both hands, she practiced swinging it like she was trying to hit a home run. In her travels as a crack fiend she'd ran into plenty of other junkies who'd tried to rob her for the merchandise she'd salvaged, or the profit she'd made turning it in. Ever since then, she'd made it a habit to bring along her trusty baseball bat which she affectionately named Lucinda. In addition to carrying *Lucinda*, Ms. Jones also carried a knife for backup which she kept strapped to her leg.

After sliding her knife in the sheath strapped to her leg, Ms. Jones headed for her bedroom door. She was going to get her shopping cart from out of the garage and hit the streets to see what she could come up on. As soon as she opened her bedroom door, she found herself standing in front of two muscle-bound goons wearing black ski-masks and black T-shirts. She swung her baseball bat at one of them, and he ducked it. He punched her in the stomach, and she doubled over, holding herself. He then followed up with an uppercut which lifted her off her feet and dropped her on the bed. She lay upon the bed with her eyes rolled back in her head. She brought her head up and saw four of the goons when there were only actually two. Sensing her life was in danger, she lifted up her jean leg to grab her knife. She'd pulled it halfway out, when the goon that assaulted her grabbed her wrist and pried it from her frail hand.

The goon threw the knife aside and roughly turned Ms. Jones over on her stomach. He pulled out a length of rope seemingly out of thin air and used it to restrain her wrists behind her back. The other goon stepped forward with a bandana to gag her mouth with, and a black pillowcase. Once he secured the gag around her mouth, he pulled the black pillowcase over her head and hoisted her over his shoulder. He motioned for his partner to follow him, and they walked through the house. They made it out the back door and across the dirt patch lawn. They approached the rear double doors of an old black van with rust spots on it. A short Mexican man was standing at the back of the van. He had a hood on his head, black sunglasses and a blue bandana tied over his nose and mouth. Gun at his side, he opened the double doors for the goons, seeing them coming his way.

The short Mexican man stood aside, as the goons tossed Ms. Jones into the back of the van. Once the goons had climbed in behind her, he slammed the double doors shut and walked over to the driver side door. He climbed inside, behind the wheel, and slammed the door shut behind him. He stashed his gun underneath the seat and pulled his hood from over his head. Next, he removed his sunglasses and set them aside on the front passenger seat. He pulled the bandana down from over the lower half of his face. Holding his cellular in his glove hand, he held on to the steering wheel and cranked the van back up. As he drove down the alleyway, he hit up his boss to give him a report on the mission he'd sent him on.

"What's up, big bro? This Tec. Yeah," he smiled as he steered with one hand and held the cell phone to his ear with the other. "I picked up that lil' package for you and I'm on my way to drop it off—"

***

Ms. Jones stirred awake and looked at what she was wearing. She was wearing an apron over her bra and panties. Feeling something snug around her neck, she touched it and felt a leather strap. She managed to slip her fingers underneath it, and tugged on it, but it wouldn't come loose. She felt around the strap and came across a small black device attached to it. Slowly, she got upon her feet and turned around in a three-hundred-sixty degree circle, scanning her surroundings. She was inside of the sleeping quarters of Joaquin's super lab. There was a fifty-inch flat-screen on every wall, bunk beds lined up on either side of the room, alongside lockers and a huge bathroom just on the other side of it.

Oh, my god, this can't be true! This must be a nightmare! It's gotta be—it's gotta be a nightmare! This cannot be happening to me again, Ms. Jones thought, as she clutched either side of her head, with her eyes bulging. The old crackhead spun around in circles over and over again, going mad. She believed she was inside of the Twilight Zone and she'd never be able to escape it.

Right then, two guards entered the sleeping quarters, armed with machine guns. They slowly moved in on Ms. Jones, as she turned around in circles faster and faster until she eventually dropped to the floor. She balled into a fetus position, still clutching her head. Her eyes were wide, and she was repeating gibberish over and over again. She looked and acted like she'd been driven completely insane.

"What the fuck is wrong with this bitch?" one of the guards asked the other.

"I don't know, but her cracked-out-ass is gon' have to snap outta it and get to work!" the other guard said.

***

Mexico: Night

Ignacio smoked a cigar as he stood in his backyard, staring down at two tombstones. The tombstones belonged to his deceased mother and father, Griselda and Mateo

Torres—both of whom he murdered in cold blood! Ignacio clenched down on his cigar and unzipped his pants, pulling his flaccid dick free from captivity. He aimed his penis at his father's tombstone. Two squirts of piss came out, and then the urine flowed in full-force splashing against Mateo's tombstone. A smile went across Ignacio's lips, as he swung his meat over to his mother's tombstone. He pissed on it until his bladder was completely empty. He then shook the piss leaking from his pee-hole and put it back up, zipping up his pants.

"Que ambos descansen en la orina! (*May you both rest in piss!*)" Ignacio said and took the cigar out of his mouth, spitting on both of their tombstones. He then looked up at the moon as it shone in the dark sky above. "You're back—I hope you've come bearing good news," Ignacio spoke to Madrid without turning around to him. He then flicked what was left of his cigar aside and sent embers flying. His forehead indented with lines when he finally turned around to Madrid, seeing the gauze taped down over the side of his neck and his bandaged hand. "What happened up there?" he questioned with curiosity. He honestly didn't give a fuck what happened to Madrid; he was just nosy.

"Returning with your prize wasn't an easy task as you may have believed. You must have forgotten Joaquin was under my tutelage. I taught that kid everything he knows, and it seems he's picked up a couple of tricks of his own since he's been away." Madrid said those words straight up. "Still, when it comes to youth versus experience—I'm living proof of what shall always prevail." He spoke arrogantly, tapping his bandaged hand against his chest, wearing a hard face.

Ignacio nodded and a smile spread across his face. "You're the best there is at what chu do, Madrid. That's why

I hired you." He focused his eyes on the duffle bag that Madrid held in his hand. He licked his lips and rubbed his hands together in anticipation of what was inside. "Is that what I think it is inside of that bag?"

Madrid cracked a one-sided grin and said, "You assumed correctly. Come have a look." He motioned him over, and he approached. Ignacio stared down at the duffle bag, excited as he continued to rub his hands together. His trifling ass couldn't wait to see Joaquin's severed head. He'd already picked out the space on the shelf where he was going to put it once he'd had it dipped in gold.

Madrid held the duffle bag as Ignacio unzipped it. Holding both sides of the duffle bag open, he peered inside and a confused expression etched across his face. The only thing inside of the duffle bag was a big long ass machete.

"What the fuck is—" the rest of Ignacio's words died in his throat. Madrid had snatched the machete out of the duffle bag and slammed its hilt into his face. The impact broke his nose, and blood gushed out of it. Ignacio slapped his hands over his bleeding nostrils, as he staggered backward. Awkwardly, he took a step back and fell on his ass.

Keeping his eyes on him, Madrid whistled, and all of the goons that worked for Ignacio poured in on either side of him. Madrid had informed them of how Ignacio had set up Mateo and Griselda to be murdered and blamed it on Joaquin, just so he could be acting boss. The goons had mad love for Mateo, so they were pissed off and looking to avenge his death.

"You're a sneaky, trifling, backstabbing, malevolent piece of shit, you know that?" Madrid told him as he stood at the head of the pack of goons. "I bet chu thought no one would ever find out what you did to your mother and father, didn't you? Well, surprise, gilipollas, 'cause we know all about it. From now on, I'll be the jefe of the Blood Brothers." He passed the machete and the duffle bag to Nolan who was Griselda's personal bodyguard before she was murdered. Nolan tossed the duffle bag over to one of the goons and pulled his long hair back into a ponytail, tangling a rubber band around it. He then twirled the machete around his hand as he advanced in Ignacio's direction with an evil look in his eyes. "And as far as Joaquin's head going up on that shelf in your, well, *my* study—don't worry—'cause your head is going to replace it."

Ignacio looked around at Madrid, Nolan and the goons, wide eyed and terrified, blood dripping off his chin. He backed away from them on his hands and the heels of his shoes as they walked toward him. Fearing for his life, he scrambled back upon his feet and took off running. Glancing over his shoulder and seeing Nolan chasing after him, he ran faster, trying to evade his impending capture. He could hear the former bodyguard's hurried footsteps getting closer and closer behind him. Before he knew it, fire ripped through his Achilles tendon, and he felt an excruciating pain. His face balled up in agony, and he took a nose dive to the ground. He tried to get up on the leg he'd felt the pain in, but he fell back to the ground. That's when he realized that his Achilles tendon had been severed. Looking over his shoulder, he saw Nolan speed-walking in his direction, droplets of blood falling from the end of his machete.

Ignacio's eyes bulged with terror, and his mouth hung open. He hopped upon his good leg and hobbled forward as fast as he could. He huffed and puffed, feeling sweat drench his face and wet the collar of his shirt. Glancing over his shoulder, he saw Nolan closing the distance between them, so he hobbled faster.

"Oh, shit! Oh, shit! Oh, shit!" Ignacio said over and over

again. He knew he was in danger, but that wasn't going to stop him from trying to escape his looming doom. "Aaaaaaah!" He threw his head back, screaming so loudly in excruciation that the little pink thing at the back of his throat vibrated crazily. He collapsed to the ground and noticed he couldn't get upon his feet, no matter how hard he tried. It dawned on him that Nolan had severed his other Achilles tendon. Suddenly, he started crying, and clear green snot oozed out of his nose, his bottom lip quivering. He prayed to the Almighty Lord in Spanish, as he desperately tried to crawl away from the Mexican Grim Reaper. When he felt a foot stomp down upon his back, Ignacio sobbed harder and harder, drenching his face with tears. His tears mixed with his snot and hung off his chin in two slimy ropes.

"Y adónde diablos crees que vas? (*And where in the fuck do you think you're going?*)" Nolan asked with his foot firmly planted on his back and his bloody machete held at his side. Using his foot, he pushed Ignacio over on his back and looked down at him. Although he was a pretty boy, he had the ugliest wettest, slimiest face right then, with his hands together pleadingly.

"Please, don't kill me, bro! I beg of you, show mercy! I don't wanna die! I don't wanna die!" Ignacio cried like a newborn baby that had been pulled from its mother's womb. It was a really sad sight to see a grown-ass man reduced to snot and tears like a goddamn toddler.

"Shut the fuck up, and take it like a man, you fucking pussy!" Nolan snarled and kicked Ignacio in the mouth, bloodying his grill, sending broken teeth flying across the ground. He laid with the side of his head on the surface, sobbing hard and loud, hating what was to come.

Right then, the goons surrounded Nolan and Ignacio while Madrid watched from a safe distance. He could hear

Ignacio's blood-curdling screams, as Nolan hacked away at his body.

"Raaaaaah! Raaahhh!" Ignacio screamed in unbearable pain. "Please, please, no, no—Aaaaah!—" His voice trailed off, and the sound of Nolan's machete could be heard chopping away at his warm flesh.

Madrid couldn't actually see what was happening, but he could most definitely hear it. Suddenly, something was thrown out of the middle of the surrounding goons. It went high up into the air and landed on the ground at Madrid's foot. He looked down and saw Ignacio's severed arm. When he looked back up, he saw the rest of the pretty boy's limbs being thrown out of the goons' circle, landing wherever they pleased. Ignacio continued to scream and holler the entire time.

"Aaaaah! Aaaaaaah! Aaaaaaaah!"

Ignacio's screams abruptly went silent after a while. It was then that Madrid figured he was undoubtedly dead.

The goons parted like the Red Sea, and Nolan came strolling out of the path they'd made. He casually strolled toward Madrid with splatters of blood on his face and clothing. He held his bloody machete and the duffle bag in one hand, and Ignacio's severed head in the other. As Nolan proceeded toward Madrid, he stuffed the head inside the duffle bag and zipped it up. He then wiped the sweat that dripped from his brow with his bloody hand, leaving a streak behind.

"Thank you for allowing me to do this, Madrid," Nolan said, as he passed him the duffle bag. "Mateo and Griselda can finally rest in peace now."

Madrid looked him in his eyes and gripped his shoulder, reassuringly. "Indeed they can—I'd like you to be the second acting boss of the Brothers. Are you up to the task, hermano?"

Nolan smiled hard and nodded. "Si, it would be my pleasure."

"Good," Madrid replied with a smile. He switched hands with the duffle bag and extended his hand toward Nolan. Nolan looked at Madrid's hand and then his bloody hand. "A lil' blood never hurt anyone. In fact, empires were built on it." Nolan nodded understandingly and shook his hand. Their deal had been signed in blood.

***

The next day

The afternoon was warm and the sun was exceptionally bright; its rays cast through the windows of the study that was once Ignacio's but now belonged to Madrid. Madrid, who was wearing a fedora and linen suit, was leaning back in his executive office chair with his legs crossed upon the desk top. The latest boss of the Blood Brothers Inc. Cartel twiddled his bare feet as he smoked a fat ass Cuban cigar, smoke wafting around him exotically. Shades covered his eyes, as he watched the seventy-five inch flat-screen television set mounted on the wall which a soccer game was playing on.

"Come on, come on, come on!" Madrid said excitedly as he sat up in his chair, leaning over the desk top and clenching his fists. One of the players on the team he was rooting for was making his way down the field with the white and black ball. He got about ten feet away from the goal and kicked the ball as hard as he could. The ball rocketed through the air. The guy covering the netted goal post dove to block the ball, but it flew past him, bumping into the net. "Yeaaaah!" Madrid hollered and threw his hands up in the air, joyfully. He then slammed his fist down on the desk top, rattling the portrait of him and Joaquin. "That's what I'm talking about, baby! That's what the fuck I'm talking about!" He slapped the desk top and leaned back in his chair again.

Knock, knock, knock!

"Come in!" Madrid told whoever was at the door. The door swung open, and the maid walked inside. She was an older Mexican lady wearing a powder blue and white uniform. She had a duffle bag in one hand and a duster in the other.

"Good evening, señor, I am here to dust the shelf like you requested," the maid—Katherine—told him.

Holding the cigar clenched between his teeth, Madrid motioned Katherine over to dust the bronze trophies behind him. Katherine scurried over to the shelf behind Madrid's desk, and he scooted up to give her room. She dusted the trophies off one by one, and then made a place at the very center of the top shelf.

"Señor Madrid, do you mind handing me the trophy outta that duffle bag by your foot?" Katherine asked from where she stood upon a chair in front of the shelf, outstretching her hand downward.

"No problema," Madrid said, as he sat the duffle bag upon the desk top and unzipped it. He took out another trophy, holding it between his hands.

Standing upright, Madrid extended it toward Katherine who took it from him. She placed the head at the center of the top shelf and adjusted it to Madrid's liking. She then dusted it off and climbed down from the chair with his assistance. They stood side by side, looking up at the trophy she'd just placed on the top shelf.

Smiling, Katherine looked back and forth between the trophy and Madrid. "What do you think, jefe?"

Madrid stared up at the top shelf, smiling with the cigar clenched between his teeth. "That's the most beautiful trophy of them all," he said of Ignacio's severed head sitting at the center of the top shelf. It held the mold of him with his eyes wide screaming in horror.

***

One year later

A pink-faced Judge with a big head and non-existent hairline pushed his wireframe eyeglasses back up on his nose. He gave God a verbal lashing, as his pupils burned like two balls of dry hay and the thick veins at his temples twitched. The fat-necked heavyset law official expressed his contempt and disgust with God who was standing before him in shackles and an orange jumpsuit. The crimes he had been accused of saddened and sickened him all at the same time. Once he was done chewing God's ass out, he scooted his chair closer to his desk and looked over the paperwork lying before him. He started coughing and patting his chest.

"Are you all right, your honor?" the sexy dark-skinned bailiff asked with a furrowed forehead, looking concerned about the honorable judge's well-being. She wore her individual braids pulled back and wrapped up in a bun. She was dressed in the traditional tan and green Sheriff's uniform.

"I'm fine, Vintesha, thank you—Just needa sip of water," the judge said to her, as he picked up the clear pitcher of water and poured himself a glass half full. He took a long drink, sat the glass down and wiped his mouth with a napkin. "At this time, I would like to ask that you stand—" he addressed both legal teams, and they obliged his request. "—Mr. Purdy, it is the sentence of the court that your custody be committed to the department of corrections for confinement of the California state prisons without the possibility of parole for the remainder of your life!"

The judge lifted the gavel and slammed it. The deafening sound echoed through the courtroom. The judge stood up, heading for the door. Everyone God knew from the streets, including Conrad, was in attendance at his trial. He'd blown a lot of money for his defense, but they best they could do for him was life with parole. That saved him from spending a few years on death row waiting for *The Man* to put the needle in his arm. If fate would have dealt him that hand, it would have been torturous for him in those conditions; he wasn't sure he would have hacked it. It wasn't necessarily the thought of being locked up alone, but the burden of being locked up with only his thoughts to keep him company.

God had lost his wife and his daughter, and he'd been thinking about them constantly. He loved and missed them so much that it hurt him to the core of his soul. He thought about committing suicide every day, but the gangsta in him wouldn't let him fold. On top of that he didn't want to break Conrad's heart. The old man had been holding him down for as long as he could remember. He was his street daddy, mentor and confidant; so if anything were to happen to him, he'd be sick. With all things considered, God had done so much dirt in the streets that he knew eventually it would catch up to him. He considered his incarceration as him paying his tithes to the game. The way he looked at it, every street nigga had to pay tribute to the game in some way or another. Some of them paid with time while others paid with their lives—if not both.

As God was handcuffed by the bailiff, he looked at Conrad who was perched in the front row. He acknowledged him with a smirk and a nod. Conrad stood upright and fastened the button on his suit, returning the gesture.

"I love you, boy—You hold your head in there 'cause this is not over," Conrad assured God, as he was led out of the court room. God nodded so Conrad would know he'd heard him. "We're gon' file for an appeal—I love you, Kyree! You hear me? I love you, son!" he called out louder on the tips of his expensive leather dress shoes, trying to make sure he was seen and heard.

"I love you too, unc!" God threw his head to the side and called out over his shoulder, as he and the bailiff disappeared through the door.

Once God was gone, Conrad walked out of the court room along with the rest of the people in attendance. He tried to fight back his tears, but he couldn't stop them from sliding down his cheeks. He snatched his handkerchief out of the breast pocket of his suit and dabbed his eyes, sniffling. It killed him not to cry when God had been sentenced to life imprisonment. As bad as he wanted to give in, he didn't because he knew he had to be strong for his street son. If he fell apart, he was sure God would have fallen apart too; and he couldn't allow that to happen. Although he knew God would never be a free man again, he still gave him hope. In his heart he knew that hope would keep him going while he was locked away. So he needed it more than he needed the cold hard facts.

Those cold hard facts were: God was caught at the scene of the crime with three dead bodies and a wounded little girl who'd accused him of trying to kill her. On top of that, the murder weapon had his fingerprints all over it. The D.A. had a reliable witness and enough evidence to nail God to the cross like he was Jesus. And that's exactly what they did. With the rest of his future already predicted, the most Conrad could do for him was, make sure he had plenty of money for commissary and visit him often.

Standing at the bottom of the stairs of the court building, Conrad pulled out his cellular and ordered an Uber to pick him up. He smoked a cigarette to calm his nerves until the car arrived. Seeing his ride approaching, he flicked what was left of his square aside, and hopped into the backseat. After greeting his driver, he lay back in the seat, and focused his attention out of the window. Tears filled his eyes and ran down his cheeks unevenly. A grin formed at the corner of his lips, as he watched the good times he and God shared throughout the years play out on the window. It was like he was watching live footage of their time together. It was so realistic he tried to touch it.

***

Prison: one year later

God stood on the tier, looking at his angels discretely selling his poison. Since he'd been incarcerated, he grew a beard and shoulder-length locs with traces of gray in them. He had a crown of thorns tattooed on his forehead with blood dripping from it. His hands were also inked with the same wounds Jesus Christ received when he was crucified. Besides his prison uniform, God resembled the holy figure down to the T. No wonder all the corrections officers and convicts alike called him by the Almighty creator's name.

Being locked up didn't slow God down at all. He started hustling while he was awaiting his trial in the county jail. He had niggaz that had been working for him in the streets that were facing time use their girlfriends and side bitchez as mules to move his drugs. This time, instead of just crack, he was dealing in coke and heroin. The crazy part about it was, the nigga was making more bread than he was when he was out on the streets. This was because in prison everything—including contraband—was far more expensive! God was living like royalty during his lifelong bid. He had a television set, Air Jordans, newest underwear, uniforms, and his commissary was overflowing. The nigga had the latest iPhone too. In fact, every angel under him had an iPhone and everything else he had. He made sure his people ate just like he did when he was a free man.

Mothafuckaz wouldn't let me be God in the streets, so fuck it! I became God to these niggaz behind these walls. I am the Almighty and this is my Heaven, God thought with a smile and spread his arms wide. His head was on a swivel as he looked over his Heavenly Kingdom, like the true ruler he was.

The End

Submission Guideline

Submit the first three chapters of your completed manuscript to ldpsubmissions@gmail.com, subject line: Your book's title. The manuscript must be in a .doc file and sent as an attachment. Document should be in Times New Roman, double spaced and in size 12 font. Also, provide your synopsis and full contact information. If sending multiple submissions, they must each be in a separate email.

Have a story but no way to send it electronically? You can still submit to LDP/Ca$h Presents. Send in the first three chapters, written or typed, of your completed manuscript to:

LDP: Submissions Dept

Po Box 944

Stockbridge, Ga 30281

DO NOT send original manuscript. Must be a duplicate.

Provide your synopsis and a cover letter containing your full contact information.

Thanks for considering LDP and Ca$h Presents.

Coming Soon from Lock Down Publications/Ca$h Presents

BOW DOWN TO MY GANGSTA

By **Ca$h**

TORN BETWEEN TWO

By **Coffee**

THE STREETS STAINED MY SOUL **II**

By **Marcellus Allen**

BLOOD OF A BOSS **VI**

SHADOWS OF THE GAME II

By **Askari**

LOYAL TO THE GAME **IV**

By **T.J. & Jelissa**

IF LOVING YOU IS WRONG… **III**

By **Jelissa**

TRUE SAVAGE **VIII**

MIDNIGHT CARTEL III

DOPE BOY MAGIC IV

CITY OF KINGZ II

By **Chris Green**

BLAST FOR ME **III**

A SAVAGE DOPEBOY III

CUTTHROAT MAFIA III

DUFFLE BAG CARTEL VI

By **Ghost**

A HUSTLER'S DECEIT III

KILL ZONE **II**

BAE BELONGS TO ME III

A DOPE BOY'S QUEEN III

By **Aryanna**

COKE KINGS V

KING OF THE TRAP II

By **T.J. Edwards**

GORILLAZ IN THE BAY V

3X KRAZY II

De'Kari

THE STREETS ARE CALLING II

Duquie Wilson

KINGPIN KILLAZ IV

STREET KINGS III

PAID IN BLOOD III

CARTEL KILLAZ IV

DOPE GODS III

Hood Rich

SINS OF A HUSTLA II

ASAD

KINGZ OF THE GAME VI

Playa Ray

SLAUGHTER GANG IV

RUTHLESS HEART IV

By Willie Slaughter

THE HEART OF A SAVAGE III

By Jibril Williams

FUK SHYT II

By Blakk Diamond

TRAP GOD III

By Troublesome

YAYO IV

GHOST MOB

Stilloan Robinson

KINGPIN DREAMS III

By Paper Boi Rari

CREAM II

By Yolanda Moore

SON OF A DOPE FIEND III

By Renta

FOREVER GANGSTA II

GLOCKS ON SATIN SHEETS III

By Adrian Dulan

LOYALTY AIN'T PROMISED III

By Keith Williams

THE PRICE YOU PAY FOR LOVE II

By Destiny Skai

CONFESSIONS OF A GANGSTA III

By Nicholas Lock

I'M NOTHING WITHOUT HIS LOVE II

SINS OF A THUG II

By Monet Dragun

LIFE OF A SAVAGE IV

MURDA SEASON IV

GANGLAND CARTEL III

By **Romell Tukes**

QUIET MONEY IV

THUG LIFE II

By **Trai'Quan**

THE STREETS MADE ME III

By **Larry D. Wright**

THE ULTIMATE SACRIFICE VI

IF YOU CROSS ME ONCE II

ANGEL III

By **Anthony Fields**

FRIEND OR FOE III

By **Mimi**

SAVAGE STORMS II

By **Meesha**

BLOOD ON THE MONEY III

By J-Blunt

THE STREETS WILL NEVER CLOSE II

By K'ajji

NIGHTMARES OF A HUSTLA II

By King Dream

THE WIFEY I USED TO BE II

By Nicole Goosby

IN THE ARM OF HIS BOSS

By Jamila

MONEY, MURDER & MEMORIES II

Malik D. Rice

Available Now

RESTRAINING ORDER **I & II**

By **CA$H & Coffee**

LOVE KNOWS NO BOUNDARIES **I II & III**

By **Coffee**

RAISED AS A GOON I, II, III & IV

BRED BY THE SLUMS I, II, III

BLAST FOR ME I & II

ROTTEN TO THE CORE I II III

A BRONX TALE I, II, III

DUFFLE BAG CARTEL I II III IV V

HEARTLESS GOON I II III IV

A SAVAGE DOPEBOY I II

HEARTLESS GOON I II III

DRUG LORDS I II III

CUTTHROAT MAFIA I II

By **Ghost**

LAY IT DOWN **I & II**

LAST OF A DYING BREED

BLOOD STAINS OF A SHOTTA I & II III

By **Jamaica**

LOYAL TO THE GAME I II III

LIFE OF SIN I, II III

By **TJ & Jelissa**

BLOODY COMMAS I & II

SKI MASK CARTEL I II & III

KING OF NEW YORK I II,III IV V

RISE TO POWER I II III

COKE KINGS I II III IV

BORN HEARTLESS I II III IV

KING OF THE TRAP

By **T.J. Edwards**

IF LOVING HIM IS WRONG…I & II

LOVE ME EVEN WHEN IT HURTS I II III

By **Jelissa**

WHEN THE STREETS CLAP BACK I & II III

THE HEART OF A SAVAGE I II

By **Jibril Williams**

A DISTINGUISHED THUG STOLE MY HEART I II & III

LOVE SHOULDN'T HURT I II III IV

RENEGADE BOYS I II III IV

PAID IN KARMA I II III

SAVAGE STORMS

By **Meesha**

A GANGSTER'S CODE I &, II III

A GANGSTER'S SYN I II III

THE SAVAGE LIFE I II III

CHAINED TO THE STREETS I II III

BLOOD ON THE MONEY I II

By J-Blunt

PUSH IT TO THE LIMIT

By **Bre' Hayes**

BLOOD OF A BOSS **I, II, III, IV, V**

SHADOWS OF THE GAME

By **Askari**

THE STREETS BLEED MURDER **I, II & III**

THE HEART OF A GANGSTA I II& III

By **Jerry Jackson**

CUM FOR ME I II III IV V VI

An **LDP Erotica Collaboration**

BRIDE OF A HUSTLA **I II & II**

THE FETTI GIRLS **I, II& III**

CORRUPTED BY A GANGSTA I, II III, IV

BLINDED BY HIS LOVE

THE PRICE YOU PAY FOR LOVE

DOPE GIRL MAGIC I II III

By **Destiny Skai**

WHEN A GOOD GIRL GOES BAD

By **Adrienne**

THE COST OF LOYALTY I II III

By Kweli

A GANGSTER'S REVENGE **I II III & IV**

THE BOSS MAN'S DAUGHTERS I II III IV V

A SAVAGE LOVE **I & II**

BAE BELONGS TO ME I II

A HUSTLER'S DECEIT I, II, III

WHAT BAD BITCHES DO I, II, III

SOUL OF A MONSTER I II III

KILL ZONE

A DOPE BOY'S QUEEN I II

By **Aryanna**

A KINGPIN'S AMBITON

A KINGPIN'S AMBITION **II**

I MURDER FOR THE DOUGH

By **Ambitious**

TRUE SAVAGE I II III IV V VI VII

DOPE BOY MAGIC I, II, III

MIDNIGHT CARTEL I II

CITY OF KINGZ

By **Chris Green**

A DOPEBOY'S PRAYER

By **Eddie "Wolf" Lee**

THE KING CARTEL **I, II & III**

By **Frank Gresham**

THESE NIGGAS AIN'T LOYAL **I, II & III**

By **Nikki Tee**

GANGSTA SHYT **I II &III**

By **CATO**

THE ULTIMATE BETRAYAL

By **Phoenix**

BOSS'N UP **I , II & III**

By **Royal Nicole**

I LOVE YOU TO DEATH

By Destiny J

I RIDE FOR MY HITTA

I STILL RIDE FOR MY HITTA

By **Misty Holt**

LOVE & CHASIN' PAPER

By **Qay Crockett**

TO DIE IN VAIN

SINS OF A HUSTLA

By **ASAD**

BROOKLYN HUSTLAZ

By **Boogsy Morina**

BROOKLYN ON LOCK I & II

By **Sonovia**

GANGSTA CITY

By **Teddy Duke**

A DRUG KING AND HIS DIAMOND I & II III

A DOPEMAN'S RICHES

HER MAN, MINE'S TOO I, II

CASH MONEY HO'S

THE WIFEY I USED TO BE

By Nicole Goosby

TRAPHOUSE KING **I II & III**

KINGPIN KILLAZ I II III

STREET KINGS I II

PAID IN BLOOD **I II**

CARTEL KILLAZ I II III

DOPE GODS I II

By **Hood Rich**

LIPSTICK KILLAH **I, II, III**

CRIME OF PASSION I II & III

FRIEND OR FOE I II

By **Mimi**

STEADY MOBBN' **I, II, III**

THE STREETS STAINED MY SOUL

By **Marcellus Allen**

WHO SHOT YA **I, II, III**

SON OF A DOPE FIEND I II

Renta

GORILLAZ IN THE BAY **I II III IV**

TEARS OF A GANGSTA I II

3X KRAZY

DE'KARI

TRIGGADALE I II III

Elijah R. Freeman

GOD BLESS THE TRAPPERS I, II, III

THESE SCANDALOUS STREETS I, II, III

FEAR MY GANGSTA I, II, III IV, V

THESE STREETS DON'T LOVE NOBODY I, II

BURY ME A G I, II, III, IV, V

A GANGSTA'S EMPIRE I, II, III, IV

THE DOPEMAN'S BODYGAURD I II

THE REALEST KILLAZ I II III

Tranay Adams

THE STREETS ARE CALLING

Duquie Wilson

MARRIED TO A BOSS… I II III

By Destiny Skai & Chris Green

KINGZ OF THE GAME I II III IV V

Playa Ray

SLAUGHTER GANG I II III

RUTHLESS HEART I II III

By Willie Slaughter

FUK SHYT

By Blakk Diamond

DON'T F#CK WITH MY HEART I II

By Linnea

ADDICTED TO THE DRAMA I II III

IN THE ARM OF HIS BOSS II

By Jamila

YAYO I II III

A SHOOTER'S AMBITION I II

By S. Allen

TRAP GOD I II

By Troublesome

FOREVER GANGSTA

GLOCKS ON SATIN SHEETS I II

By Adrian Dulan

TOE TAGZ I II III

By Ah'Million

KINGPIN DREAMS I II

By Paper Boi Rari

CONFESSIONS OF A GANGSTA I II

By Nicholas Lock

I'M NOTHING WITHOUT HIS LOVE

SINS OF A THUG

By Monet Dragun

CAUGHT UP IN THE LIFE I II III

By Robert Baptiste

NEW TO MONEY, MURDER & MEMORIES

THE GAME I II III

By **Malik D. Rice**

LIFE OF A SAVAGE I II III

A GANGSTA'S QUR'AN I II III

MURDA SEASON I II III

GANGLAND CARTEL I II

By **Romell Tukes**

LOYALTY AIN'T PROMISED I II

By Keith Williams

QUIET MONEY I II III

THUG LIFE

By **Trai'Quan**

THE STREETS MADE ME I II

By **Larry D. Wright**

THE ULTIMATE SACRIFICE I, II, III, IV, V

KHADIFI

IF YOU CROSS ME ONCE

ANGEL I II

By **Anthony Fields**

THE LIFE OF A HOOD STAR

By Ca$h & Rashia Wilson

THE STREETS WILL NEVER CLOSE

By K'ajji

CREAM

By Yolanda Moore

NIGHTMARES OF A HUSTLA

By King Dream

BOOKS BY LDP'S CEO, CA$H

TRUST IN NO MAN

TRUST IN NO MAN 2

TRUST IN NO MAN 3

BONDED BY BLOOD

SHORTY GOT A THUG

THUGS CRY

THUGS CRY 2

THUGS CRY 3

TRUST NO BITCH

TRUST NO BITCH 2

TRUST NO BITCH 3

TIL MY CASKET DROPS

RESTRAINING ORDER

RESTRAINING ORDER 2

IN LOVE WITH A CONVICT

LIFE OF A HOOD STAR

CPSIA information can be obtained
at www.ICGtesting.com
Printed in the USA
LVHW010413260821
696090LV00020B/1849